IF ONLY PEOPLE WERE LIKE HORSES

BY STEPHEN ROCCO

This is a work of fiction. Names, characters, places and incidents are either the product of the author's imagination or are used fictitiously. Any resemblance to actual persons, living or dead, businesses, companies, events or locales is entirely coincidental.

"If Only People Were Like Horses," by Stephen Rocco. ISBN 978-1-63868-187-8 (softcover).

Published 2025 by Virtualbookworm.com Publishing, P.O. Box 9949, College Station, TX 77842, US.

This book is dedicated to Florence and Silvio Ricci

"United with Steven Michael in Heaven"

Also by Stephen Rocco

From Conflict to Cooperation: Succeed with Rocco's 4 R's

The Mystery in the Mausoleum

The Ecstasy of Pupusas, Filled with Love

The Girl Who Woke Up in the Morgue

Prologue

I OBSERVE AS AN EIGHT-LEGGED ARTHROPOD meticulously designs a silk prison. Each appendage seamlessly creates a den of death in my prison cell. "A prison within a prison", I mutter.

Out of this gangly architect's reach I would never have appreciated its talents. Just like I never appreciated the art or ability of anyone but myself. Prison will do wonders for your mental clarity, when your body is told what to do. Yes, amidst flushing toilets, echoes of flatulence, and the occasional cry of "Mama," I, Steven Ricci, have found wisdom.

All those years my poor mother Carole was wrong. "You're too smart for your own good, Steven," was her lament, as she normally reached for another cigarette and pondered how she would get me out of one of my escapades. "If only your father was around," was another, although I did not feel the same way. The dads I saw yelled things like, "Johnny run faster! …Pat, what's wrong with you?... Charlie, why can't you do better?" Na, I was fine without a dad. My mother should have said, "Steven get some wisdom." Shit, I knew I was smart. All those guidance counselors loved to wave my high I.Q. scores in my face. "You're capable of so much more….blah, blah."

But to acquire wisdom one has to peel away the layers of blame, arrogance and selfishness that define a “special person”. I thought I had done that years ago in an earlier imprisonment. But I see now I was wrong. I made the same selfish mistakes again.

See, I always felt special. Even as a child I had a natural ability to motivate the weak, the greedy and even good kids. Rules don’t apply to special people. They don’t have to be good sons, good husbands or good fathers. They don’t have to respect those who help them achieve success. They can satisfy their own needs and use money or power to correct life’s inescapable detours that impede those who are not special.

When the inevitable fall occurs to special people, they die alone or in my case, end up in prison. The love and affection that I trampled, kicked at like dry leaves on a fall day, lay forsaken. I am now wise enough to say I’m sorry, but to whom – my hubris echoes, “He got what he deserved.”

In my nocturnal self-discovery, I realize my only affection for another beside myself was not a person, but an animal. In my pleasant mirage I stroke the black mane of Rumi Rose. I feel her long wooly muzzle affectionately digging into my shirt for more sugar. From my first gaze, the outside of a horse made me feel better inside. I can’t explain it otherwise. If loving people was as easy, I would not be staring at spiders in my prison cell. This is the story of a horse lover who was not special, and not wise until now.

Chapter 1: The Young Life of a Special Person

THE KIND EYES of the kindergarten teacher welcoming her brood of cherubic youngsters turned dark when Steven entered the classroom. After one month the five year old Steven had successfully caused this just-graduated, exuberant teacher to reconsider her career choice. Steven seemed to know that and it did not bother him one bit.

He had seen those same eyes in his mother's stare. Steven did not intend to hurt other people, but if you were in his world you were going to bump into him. From an early age Steven always felt he was the center of the world. He saw people moving around him and to him they were like cars moving in and out of a traffic jam. He was the manipulator of their actions.

Some kids are nervous or intimated by adults. Not Steven. Even as a five year old, Steven might ask the variety shop owner, "Why do you charge so much for chocolate," or using his natural skills of persuasion, "How about giving a kid who lost his dad in the war some free candy Mister?"

More than once his poor single parent mother asked, "Where did you come from?" As he got older, it became the rhetorical, "You're too smart for your own good!" Steven was just different than most kids. Fatherless, he never asked about his father Phillip Ricci, or the circumstances of his death. He heard that his father was a Marine who died in Vietnam, and that was enough.

But occasionally, when his mom was not around he would pick up the framed photo of his dad which was gathering dust in the corner of the living room. Steven would hold the photo beside his face, while looking into a mirror. He would mimic the determined face of the ramrod straight Marine facing him. The vacant stare and the curled lip of the Marine conveyed no emotion. But there was familiarity in the sandy hair, deep green tea eyes, and lean cheeks descending to a firm, "Don't mess with me" jaw. Pleasant daydreaming lasted only so long with Steven, who always quickly put away his dad's photo with the dust intact.

Steven realizes now that he possessed a lot of anger which he took out on other people. His anger was dangerous for a couple of reasons. He was smart – he could read at the age of five - but he was smarter about people. As if by instinct he could detect the tiniest cues – the doubts, the poor self-esteem, the hidden passions – and motivate others to join him in his exploits.

For example, in the first week of kindergarten he invented a game called, "The Whip." He got other sweet faced boys to join hands and straight arm innocent girls on the playground. Some boys hesitated; others promptly followed Steven's lead to act in a way they would never choose to do on their own. Even the terrified girls who did not get "Whipped" fell to the ground. The poor teacher had a roomful of muddy tattered dresses and weepy faces.

For the boys who would not join Steven's gang, he invented another game, "Tennis Ball." Reluctant five- and six-year-olds would be chased by charging Steven and his gang, and hit with multiple balls until they cried.

It wasn't long before the familiar clickety-clack of his mother's high heels followed him through his formative years of school. An elegant long-legged forty something, Carole Ricci was well known in Arcadia, Kentucky. The widow of a Marine hero, she worked as an administrator for the town's fire department. Always voguish, she never went out unless her hair, face, and nails were perfect. In fact, many of Arcadia's "finest" dated Carole. The men in her life rarely lasted more than one date. Steven's favorite sabotage was letting the air out of these men's car tires. Appearances mattered to Carole Ricci, and her son Steven did not help her image.

Steven would sit politely, as his mother, handkerchief in hand, promised the principals at various schools, "He just made a mistake, he will try harder." Perfect people watcher that he was, Steven would sit admiring his mother's performance. For he knew deep down his mother had thrown up her hands a long time ago. By seventh grade he was put in an "alternative" school which means he did nothing. Some Arcadia loser would be assigned to babysit the students, who read comic books for five to six hours per day. This gave Steven Ricci plenty of time to develop hijinks.

By age twelve Steven had put together his own gang of like-minded delinquents. They continued one of his impressive schemes he initially started in second grade. Many modern criminals use it today. Steven labeled it "The Swarm." It started at the local candy store owned by a kindly couple who bought the store in their retirement. Six youngsters would raid the store, grab as much candy as they could, and run away in six different directions.

Steven dominated a like-minded friend Raymond, who was as close to Steven as anyone was allowed. Soon Steven and Raymond had graduated to stealing radios, C D's, and anything else they could find in unlocked cars. Their latest "swarming" scam had taken place at a local camera-electronic store operated by a one-legged man – the Doyle of Doyle Electronics.

For once Steven was outsmarted by this fat, old man, only known as Doyle. As Steven's criminal team scooped and grabbed cameras and tech goods, Doyle, with his round face, big belly and one leg sat by calmly. When Steven hollered, "Let's go," the door would not budge. The next thing Steven felt was a gun pressed to his forehead. "You the leader here?" Steve surprised himself and answered, "Yeah." Then everything went black.

He awoke to three boys, and a smiling Doyle surrounding him. Steven vaguely remembered two of the boys from school who were several years older than him. "Should we kill him?" said one of the boys.

Again, Steven remained composed. "I guess I picked the wrong place."

"You sure did," said the leader of this older group, as he kicked Steven in the gut. Steven lost his breath but did not cry.

Doyle, looking around at his boys, spoke next, "You guys are getting a bit big for the house jobs. Nicky over here is getting a bit too big." Steven vaguely remembered the fellow known as Nicky – yes Nicky Bianco. The diminutive Nicky, chewing on a toothpick did not say a word.

"What do you have in mind Doyle?" said another boy.

"He's small enough to get into some of the mansions on the south side Robbie. He's got balls, if nothing else."

And that's how Steven became a member of an older criminal gang. They used Steven to get into basement windows, and Doyle taught him to disable alarms. Even stoic Doyle gave Steven a compliment, "You pick up the alarm stuff pretty quick kid."

Weekends were spent patrolling rich neighborhoods for easy robberies. Robbie, the leader of the group went for easy pickings. "Let's get the house where the rich fucks are enjoying their vacations." They tried to rob one house each weekend. Doyle was the fence who would give them 50% of their total score of jewelry, furs, televisions, and computers.

Soon Steven was socializing with these older boys. Not intimidated by these "partners in crime", Steven began smoking marijuana and carousing with his new friends. His mother eventually gave up questioning why these older youths were picking up her fifteen year old son in a car night after night; just like she stopped questioning how Steven had hundred dollar bills stuffed into the pockets of his dirty jeans. And she had nothing to say when Steven made the decision to simply stop going to his alternative school. "It's just for dummies Ma."

Over the next two years, Steven and his crew hung out at the local pool hall. There they socialized and planned their next robberies. Now, nearly six feet tall, Steven had his first sexual experience with a girl about his own age, who hung around to get free pot from Robbie and his gang. Steven was growing up fast and thought nothing unusual about his life.

One day Steven found himself playing pool with the fellow whom he suspected once asked Doyle if Steven should be killed. Nicky Bianco could have been a miniature version of Michaelangelo's "David". Barely five foot two inches, he was perfectly proportioned with large muscular forearms and a formidable chest. Dark, buoyant curls framed a Neapolitan countenance – large nose, chestnut eyes, and an oval face.

"I'm getting out of this racket," spit Nicky as he racked ball after ball with his long slender fingers guiding the cue. I'm gonna go to California and become a jockey."

"I always liked horses," was Steven's response.

As Nicky lined up the eight ball to complete his victory, he stopped. "I heard your dad died in an accident."

"No, my father died in Vietnam."

"That's not what I heard. I heard he was a bad guy."

Ordinarily, a son would get angry at these words against his father. But since Steven rarely thought of his father, he felt no anger. He was more perplexed as to why Nicky even cared about his father.

"Whatever, just shoot the ball."

With that Nicky slammed the eight ball into its home and threw the cue on the table. "Game over."

Ironically, Nicky disappeared from the crew after this strange encounter. One of the boys told Steven that Nicky went to California. "He'll be back soon," he said.

Eventually the ambitious Steven realized that he did not need Robbie and his crew to succeed as a thief. He started his own gang with Raymond and two other young followers. He showed them how to case homes, especially ones where the owners were away. The clever Steven held "classes" in alarm disabling for his gang of young crooks. He found a different fence than Doyle with easier terms, and Steven branched out to rob homes in the nearby towns.

Steven's run of good luck in the house robbing business ran cold six months after he ventured out with his new crew. Alarmed by the rise in property crimes, the police in nearby Lincoln increased their surveillance in affluent neighborhoods. Steven and his boys fell right into a cop car blockade as they drove away from a heist.

At the police station Sargeant Dennis McCloud informed the seventeen year old Steven that he was to be charged with several felonies as an adult. His crew of fifteen to sixteen year old's would be treated as minors.

Years later, when thinking about the renowned horse trainer, Steven Ricci, Sgt. McCloud would recall the brash youngster who was as cool as a cucumber. "Aren't I entitled to a phone call to my attorney?" were Steven's first words. Sgt. McCloud later employed the "good cop, bad cop" routine. Steven called them out on it. "Guys you can hit me on the head or counsel me like a priest if you want, but first let me offer you a deal."

Steven then enticed the cops with his knowledge of a large robbery ring in the area. After a period of negotiations, McCloud agreed to drop all the charges against Steven for information about the Robbie/Doyle ring. Steven then provided detailed statements on how the robberies were planned and how the property was fenced. He named everyone in his former gang, including Nicky Bianco.

After indictments were handed down and arrests were made, Steven realized he had better leave the area. He headed out to Lexington, Kentucky, a city about two hours away. He left his mother a message, "Ma had to leave for a while. Call you later."

Chapter 2: Horse Wonders

THE YOUNG STEVEN HUNG AROUND Lexington's pool halls for a couple of weeks. His ill-gotten money was running out. His squat landlady with bad teeth reminded him that weekly rent for the closet sized drab room with was due next week.

Then he remembered the "Temple." Templeton racetrack in Lexington was one of the most prestigious tracks in the country. Arcadia, where Steven grew up, had a racetrack that was like the little brother of the Templeton. Arcadia raced less prestigious horses with purses often in the $3,000 - $4,000 dollar range. Arcadia was often used by Templeton's horse trainers to school young horses or to get quality horses who were injured back on their game.

Even as a boy Steven loved to peer through the fence at Arcadia and watch the horses work out. Something about a thousand pounds of regal beauty pounding the dirt softened a hard character like Steven. "Someday I'll own my own horse," Steven promised himself.

So with money running out, Steven wandered over to the "Temple" which everyone in Kentucky referred to with reverence. The rounded, blood-red brick exterior of the Temple with layers of ivy riding its arches was reminiscent of a rich man's

Roman colosseum where thoroughbreds race instead of chariots. Steven was mesmerized by the sights around him: The eager crowds inching close to one another to admire their investments. The paddock ablaze with trainers giving last minute racing instructions to their jockeys, as they hoisted themselves on their mounts. The diminutive jockeys wearing the gaudy colors of their stables, and sitting high on their horses' backs. Steven listened as two confident owners in their sear-sucker suits boasted about their horses' chances of winning to impress a slim voguish blonde. "Two rich assholes," Steven told himself as he returned to admiring the horses.

Steven followed the horses from the paddock area out to the main track. The sights almost took his breath away – admiration not a normal part of his personality. Thousands of spectators, their bible-like horse programs marked with asterisks, notes and indescribable scratches, held tightly in their hands, hooted and whistled for their favorites. Steven took notice of it all.

Standing in the middle of the crowd, Steven vaguely listened to the voices of those around him. Many claimed a solution to the riddle of which horse was the fastest.

"I always like the gray horses."

"Look at the one prancing on its toes."

"He took a dump – a great sign."

But Steven was totally absorbed in admiration of horse flesh. He was bewitched by the ten muscular athletes that danced before him. Their sweaty taut coats of chestnut gray and black sparkled in the sunlight. The long sleek necks hosting chiseled faces now bouncing up and down as if aware they were going to battle with their peers. Steven admired the powerful chests springing with transmission to the muscular hindquarters, despite their differences in size or color. While everyone else computed these nuances for profit, Steven studied their mannerisms like he did with people. *They each have their own personality*, he told himself.

In the pre-race parade, one horse in particular got Steven's attention. Looking at a neighbor's program he saw the name Rumi Rose – the number 6 horse. Running to the betting window, without even looking at the odds on the horse, Steven put his last $20 on Rumi Rose.

What did he see? Among all of the magnificent horses, Rumi's shiny penny coat reminded him of copper steel. Rumi pranced before the crowd as if engaging the audience in a theatrical performance. *It's as if she is saying watch me perform,* thought Steven.

Hearing the trumpet heralding the start of the race, Steven, holding tightly to his $20 investment ticket, rushed to the rail in time to witness the opening of the starting gate. Ten thousand pounds of starting horseflesh soon settled into ten positions on the first turn. At this point Rumi was already five lengths in the lead. Midway through the race, Rumi had opened a seventh length lead as three horses battled behind her to close the gap.

But then something unusual happened. In the final turn Rumi's stride seemed to shorten with each step. His eyes glued to the horse, Steven thought, *It's as if she decided to walk instead of run.* Similarly, the three horses fighting for position behind Rumi also seemed to tire out. Rumi's lead was reduced to three lengths as the last place horse, number 5, energy in hand, closed the gap. Steven quickly looked at his program and saw the number 5 horse was Dee-Rico. As the disparate bettors who had money on these two contenders tried to chortle their horse to victory, Steve observed an anomaly in Rumi Rose. As if playing with her opponent Rumi pulled ahead by a length only to allow Dee-Rico to pull even with her. The cheers of the frenzied crowd grew louder as these two magnificent creatures continued fighting head-to-head to the finish line. Steven perceived Rumi falter. Dee-Rico won by a nose.

Amidst the groans and cheers of the bettors, Steven did not go to the winner's circle to see the accolades given to Dee-Rico. He raced to the area where the other nine horse losers met up with their unfortunate staff of owners and trainers. There he saw a stout gentleman wearing a worn raincoat on a sunny day. The man grabbed the bridle of Rumi Rose and seemed to whisper in the horse's ear. Steven again saw the serene command of the horse, who acted like she had won the race. *I don't think the horse wanted to win the race*, believed Steven.

His pockets now empty, Steven contemplated his future. He would not be a popular person back in Arcadia. He couldn't go home.

When he arrived back at his shabby apartment, his witch of a landlord had changed his lock and put his meager belongings in a paper bag. After being turned away from an overcrowded homeless shelter, he started wandering the streets of Lexington. And then an idea came to him, *Why don't I go over to Templeton?* Behind the track he had seen row upon row of sheds, hidden from the nearby grandeur. He had observed the gritty workers who seemed invisible to the patrons of Templeton. *Maybe I can get a job there*, he thought.

So, that night, the full moon his only light, Steven roamed the solitary horse barns. His paper bag belongings as his pillow, he nestled in a stall with hay as his mattress.

Chapter 3: The "Mucker"

STEVEN AWOKE AT PRE-DAWN to a splash of hay hitting his head. "What do we have here, a trespasser?" said the salty speaker, rake in hand.

"I came here last night looking for work."

"Do you always go for a job interview in the middle of the night?"

Steven rose sneezing as he pushed the chaff out of his nose. He now towered over the raker – a full head over the slight built man. "My name is Steven Ricci. How do I get a job here?"

"It depends. You got to go see Pops. Come with me. My name is Owen Nash, but everyone calls me Owie."

As Steven walked he observed that the empty city of last night was now a dynamic metropolis. Men and women in look-a-like faded jeans, muddy boots and tattered shirts scurried about, walking horses, cleaning tubs and raking hay. Even the horses seemed to know an encroacher was in their midst. Steven felt the eyes of both horses and workers upon him as he walked with his bag of possessions in hand. Owie seemed to be in charge, calling out orders to the diverse work brigade as he walked with Steven.

"Charlie muck stalls six and seven. Sue get the feed tubs ready. Larry make sure the tack room is cleaned up, got a lot galloping today."

Steven squinted as the sunrise illuminated shadowy forms of horses and riders moving about him. "Watch it kid!" called out a faceless form astride a horse. An odd pungent sweet-sour fragrance – part hay, part manure – irritated Steven's nostrils. He passed hundreds of squat, army-like barracks. He later learned this area was called "shed row" on the backside to the track.

Owie stopped in front of one of these sheds. A mud-covered shingle, which was once an office sign, hung over the door. Steven immediately recognized the man inside. He was the same fellow who had whispered in the ear of Rumi Rose on race day.

"What do we have here, Owie?" asked Pops.

"Don't know boss. Found him in stall 46 this morning sleeping on hay."

Steven warily gazed at the pumpkin-like face of this stranger with chins for a neck. His gaze rested on the older man's intense blue eyes, which should have been eclipsed by the thick glasses resting on his nose.

"What brings you here kid? Running away from the law?"

Caught off guard by the accuracy of Pops's statement, Steven stammered, "I like horses. I would like to work with them."

"You're too big to be a jockey kid," smirked Pops, ushered by eyes that now seemed playful to Steven.

"I think I understand them." This was probably the most honest answer Steven had ever given to someone with authority over him.

"Oh, we got a horse whisperer here. You like horses more than people, do ya?"

Steven was silent but didn't know if Pops was that prescient.

"How old are you kid?"

Steven lied, "Eighteen sir."

Turning to his foreman, Pops said, "What do you think, Owie?"

Owen hesitated. Prematurely bald, the jockey sized Owen had forearms too big for his body. "He looks strong enough. We'll see if he likes to work hard."

"Okay kid," said Pops. "Owie will get you some boots, and you will start like everyone else does around here, mucking stalls. Get him in one of the dorms, but first get him something to eat."

Another drab shed, from which Steven breathed in a whiff of Southern biscuits and grits, served as a kitchen. Outside, lean workers, drinking coffee, smoking cigarettes and wearing dirty jeans, sat at long picnic tables.

"Got a new worker there Owie?" said a nameless face as he looked up at Steven. "We'll see how long he lasts."

Inside, a sweaty, slightly plump woman with stiff bleach blonde hair greeted Steven with a smile.

"Sheila, get this guy one of your best omelets," instructed Owen. "He's got a long day ahead of him."

Sheila smiled at Steven, "Better looking than most of the mutts you bring in here. Sit down, kid. You like grits?"

"Yeah," Steven said with barely a smile.

Owen turned to leave. "When you're done go to shed 44. We will have you mucking out stalls there."

"Where you from kid?" asked Sheila with a twang that was from somewhere south of Kentucky.

"Cincinnati," Steven lied.

"My first husband was from there. A real asshole."

Steven questioned, "What's mucking?"

"That's where everyone starts kid. You basically clean out the horses' shit. See these animals are treated better than you and me. Each day the crap in their stalls is cleaned, and they get a fresh bed of hay. Better than the Hilton kid. Then they get their food and water tubs cleaned and prepared for the day. If you're good at that kid, they let you walk around and around the sheds with a horse until your head spins. That's called hot walking. And if you're really good kid you graduate to the tack room."

"Tack room?" asked Steven. His question was interrupted by a quartet of who appeared to be jockeys, with protective helmets, boots, and whips. Onc of those men, looking at the new worker with a sardonic grin, piped up, "Sheila are you a cook or a nurse maid?"

"Benny you will get burnt toast if you don't shut up." Surprisingly Sheila had never stopped working while counseling the new worker. She multi-tasked twenty breakfasts during their brief conversation. “Why don’t you tell Steven here what a tack room is.”

“Anything for you Sheila. New guy, tack is all the equipment that goes on the horse – bridles, reins, bits, saddles – anything you see on the horse. We call it tacking up the horse. Don’t worry kid, you probably won’t get that far.”

Steven left Sheila with a full stomach, and a slight wave and wandered among the faceless structures. Horses, some feeding or drinking on tub near their stalls, poked their heads out at the trespasser. Steven enjoyed their gaze more than those of the men and women of every ethnic group, who watched him out of the corner of their eyes.

At shed 44 he found Owen stirring a concoction of oats, barley, and corn into a large tub. “Get me some germ oil Ed,” he called to his assistant. Turning to Steven, Owen announced, “Ed will show you the ropes Steven. You will clean out all the stalls in this block.”

Steven saw that there were thirty stalls in the number 44 block. Ed threw the new worker a rake, as he spoke to Steven in broken English, “Get the stall when the horse is out.” Steven figured out the eight foot pile of smoking waste in the middle of the little city was where he was to pile all the shit he cleaned from the stalls. He watched other workers push wheel barrels full of old and new hay,and copied their habits. One of the workers ordered him to scrub out the water trough. So Steven started cleaning out the water and food troughs. Despite the hard work Steven smiled while doing his job. He loved the horses cantering about him – one even tried to kiss Steven with a muzzle of saliva.

By early afternoon, Steven was covered in sweat, but very proud that he had cleared thirty stalls. Then he heard Owen call to him harshly, "Ricci, you want the hay molded to the horses' bodies? Fold it so the horses' bellies get lots of support, and the same for the heads!" Steven knew better than to question how he was supposed to know that.

So in the next few months Steven became one of the stable hands, enabling the equine stars to make money for their rich owners. Representing the underbelly of the racing industry, this grunt labor force made everything work, but were not seen in the winner's circle. No, the elite owners and their fawning friends would not want a groom or stable hand to spoil the photo op.

Steven awoke at dawn each day to muck the stalls, and soon acquired another job as a "hot walker." Essentially, such a groom walks the horse after a morning workout or on an off day, as a form of exercise. Unlike humans, horses must cool off after a race or heavy workout, hence the walker needs to exercise him for thirty minutes or so.

On his first day as such a groom, Steven was lambasted by Owen, "Ricci, you must always walk the horse counterclockwise, just like how he runs on the track."

Steven was forced to understand horse logic mainly on his own. Another day Steven learned the hard way not to wrap the leather shank around his hand. This was only after a fractious horse took pity on him and only dragged him ten yards.

But this did not bother Steven one bit. He loved the work because he loved being around these regal animals. He seemed to have a sixth sense as to the emotional state of these equines. This was validated to a degree when his peers allowed him to prepare the feed and water tubs of fractious horses. A bite to the groom's shoulder or a kick to his shin was second nature to some of these peevish thoroughbreds. Like he did with people, Steven quickly absorbed if such a horse was having a bad day. A quick look at a horse's ears or eyes told Steven about the horse's emotions. Ears pinned close to the neck with no forward movement was a bad sign. Calm horses have a little white to their eyes. Steven watched those eyes carefully as he prepared their feed.

In those first few weeks, Steven had little interaction with Pops. The older man did educate him about horse vision, which saved Steven's hide in his early days. Pops happened by while Steven was getting a bucket behind the horse's rear leg, and quickly yelled, "Stop!" The horse's leg was poised and ready. One more step and Steven would have received a strong kick.

"Kid, horses have almost 180 degree vision in each eye. The only place they don't see well is right in front of their noses, and behind their tails. That's how they run without hitting one another."

Steven learned more about Pops from the tough workers swilling early beers at picnic tables near the canteen. Even they were amazed at Pops's ability to figure out a horse.

"He can touch a horse's leg and see what's inside."

"I've seen him get a horse that had no business being there into the winner's circle."

Such reverence was unusual for men and women who had traveled through hard lives until landing at Templeton.

This made a deep impression on Steven, who was not usually impressed by people. But it resonated because Steven had come to a clear decision. He wanted to become a horse trainer.

One day during a lull in their work, Steven surprised himself and shared this dream with Owen. Owen eyeballed Steven carefully, and said, "I'm not sure you know how much work there is. You have to be sponsored and take state exams. That's why I'm still a foreman. But if you're committed Steven, you have the best teacher in the country in Pops. He's the best in the business."

Owen then brought his 5'4" frame close to Steven. As his Nordic, balding red head leaned into Steven's chest he warned, "Just don't fuck Pops. I've seen plenty of guys like you learn everything from Pops, and then try to take his job or steal his horses. If you get licensed, get out of Templeton, and start your own career somewhere else. Pops will be proud of you."

But Steven was thinking about himself. About how special he was, special enough to figure out horses.

Chapter 4: The Genesis of a Horse Trainer

FROM THE DAY HE UTTERED a plan for his life to become a horse trainer, Steven Ricci was a man on a mission. He had to satisfy his own goals and as he had learned those first few days at Templeton, no one was going to horse-feed him. As was typical of his mindset, he would use anyone to get ahead.

By the end of his first year at Templeton he had risen as Owen's backside assistant. His rise was the result of outworking even the most tireless backside workers.

Getting up before daybreak, Steven had piled enough manure to rival a great shit pyramid of Egypt. His stalls, carefully designed for Pops's horses to play after their feed, were spotless works of art. Soon Owen taught him to prepare the feeding tubs with Pops's special brew of wheat, barley, and oats, combined with a special concoction of herbs, oils and vitamins. Astringent to the nostrils, this mixture prompted Steven to ask Owen, "Hey, what's in this brew Pops adds to the feed?"

"Don't really know Steven. Pops gives it to all his horses. He's got lots of secrets. Sometimes he will disappear into the woods and return with mushrooms and plants. All I know is he distills them and we add three ounces of this crazy smelling juice to every tub of food. They test horses after each race, and nothing is illegal in the concoction."

Early in Steven's job education, he was told to straighten out the tack room. He walked into a haphazard horse gymnasium where leather shanks, saddles built for five year olds, and metal dentures all hung from strings of wood pegs. These were the dizzying array of attachments that lead and control horses.

Steven rubbed his hand on the soft leather bridles or halters that served as the horses' head collars. He twirled the wiry reins attached from the collars to bits, which are metal plates fitted near the horses' gums. The slight pinch of the bits by a jockey serves to control the horse's speed and direction. Metal stirrups and minute saddles completed Steven's education. Steven caressed harnesses and reins that came in various sizes and conditions. Before long Owen was confident that Steven could "tack up" any horse either for a workout, a gallop or a race.

During racing days, Steven sits by the rail on the backside with binoculars. The equine athletes, eyes wide with anxiety or determination are loaded into metal gates, the jockeys arched over their necks. Then he hears the swarming pack of thunderous hoofs bumping to their favorite part of the track as they near him. The jockeys are in perfect sync on a thousand pounds of muscle, maneuvering the horses by use of reins, kicks or whips. The tense roar of the crowd and the announcer's voice stir Steven's senses. A cannonade of pounding hooves and snorting nostrils announces their presence before Steven. He sometimes hears the jockeys' calls as they pass by, "Move your horse over; Up yours mate," above the sound of whips and racing fury,

Within seconds Steven is left with explosive hindquarters leaving dust in his face. Soon the heavens crackle with anticipation as the crowd urges their horses to victory. One team, jockey and horse, synchronized like tight ballet dancers, has won. The tiny gladiator atop his proud steed now waves to the exuberant masses.

Steven took it all in; the visible pageantry and the crowd's buzz in admiration of these elegant animals; the jockey's dexterous micro-second ability to assess the competitions' and his own horses' strengths and pace adjustments; the owner's demands that he be rewarded for his equine investments, not just monetarily, but in bragging rights. Steven could feel the prosperity and fame that would come his way one day.

But all this reinforced the value of the person who was not seen by the masses – the horse trainer. Steven realized the one person who could help him obtain success was the man named Al Wilson, better known as "Pops."

In his first year at the track, Steven had little interaction with Pops. But he kept a keen eye on the diminutive, slightly plump man, who wore plaid, flannel shirts and corduroys even in the simmering heat of a Kentucky summer. Pops's face resembled a creation that a first grader might make out of clay; protruding forehead, wide cheeks, and rounded jaw all squeezed together. But these compounds melted together to resemble a beautiful facial gourd whenever Pops smiled, which was often. In fact, Pops often seemed privy to an inside joke, evidenced in lambent eyes behind thick glasses. Atop his head was a gray tam-o-chanter, and there was always something in his mouth, maybe a pipe, a piece of hay, or even a twig he picked up from the ground.

The young protégé learned a lot by observing Pops. Steven watched in amazement as Pops's leathery, thick, knuckleless hands consoled the legs of a boisterous thoroughbred. "She has 'ouchy hocks'," murmured Pops as his thick fingers traced the horse's lower leg. Owen later translated to the ignorant Steven that this meant an inflamed ankle. Another time a horse refused to gallop, pawing the ground as if pleading for help. Coming to a miracle rescue, Pops put his ear to the horse's stomach. "The animal has impacted intestines. Call the vet right away."

The vet later shook his head in amazement, "That horse had a case of colic so severe that his intestines would have burst in two days if he wasn't diagnosed."

Between chores Steven would pepper Owen with questions about Pops.

"His life is a bit of a mystery. I've been with him ten years and he never talked about any family. Some say he was part Native American, and grew up in the desert, breaking Mustangs. Others say he was just a small-time jockey out of Indiana. But no one can find any records of his wins and losses. All I know is that he knows more about racehorses than anyone I know. He cares more about these horses than he cares about most of the people around here. Can't say I blame him. Lots of people he helped screwed him."

Steven also learned a lot about Pops from looking at the walls of Templeton Racetrack. A plaque named him as five time winner of the Pinnacle award for top trainer in the Country. Photographs of Pops, his broad face bursting with fatherly pride at his horses, adorned Templeton's clubhouse walls. Pops could be seen in winning circles at top racetracks throughout the Country in his twenty-five year career. But Steven read that Pops was mainly proud of his most savored accomplishment: winning the Templeton Million, Kentucky's most renowned horse race, ten of the last fifteen years. But he had not won in the past two years. Some whispered that the old Pops had finally lost his "fast ball."

Ironically, it was Rumi Rose, the copper filly, that Steven loved at first gaze who brought him and Pops into closer contact. In his two years at Templeton, Steven had mucked Rumi's stall with more care than he did for the other forty horses in Pops' stable. Steven swore that Rumi waited for him each morning. As he approached Rumi's stall he would see her head bobs, and hear her excited snorts and whinnies. Her head went straight to his shirt pocket for her sugar fix, and remained there as Steven nestled her mane of black silk. Horse and man gazed at each other and whispered exchanges like two lovers. Steven had never had such affection for anyone, not even his mother.

One day this loving interlude was interrupted by an argument outside of Rumi's stall. Pops's mouth chewed hard on a twig, as he was berated by a tall, distinguished looking man in a fedora and copper topcoat, nearly the color of Rumi's coat.

"Pops, you fought me for running her as a two year old, and now you want to shut her down again. Crap, she cost me $350,000 Pops, and all I got is second place money."

As if ruminating with some horse god, Pops finally said, "I got to figure her out. Let me keep her out for three months."

The other man, who Steven now realized was the owner, took off his hat and wiped his brow for the clarity he needed. "Okay, Pops. We'll do it your way. But I have to get her winning or I'll drop her into the claiming ranks. I need to get something out of this horse."

Steven dropped the rake to announce his presence in Rumi's stall. The distinguished gentleman glanced at Steven without acknowledging him and huffed off. Pops's eyes twinkled, "All he cares about is his investment kid. He could care less about beautiful Rumi here. I see you spending a lot of time with Rumi. I think she likes you."

Steven stammered, "I love all your horses, but she is special. There's something about her eyes; she takes everything in. Do you think she wants to win?"

Steven's comments got a serious glance from Pops. For in the past year Steven had been formulating his own ideas about all the horses in

Pops's 40 horse stable. In some he saw the determination that separated the winners from the losers. While most had the required conformity, muscle and gait, many did not have the confidence or will to win. Sure, Steven came to realize that a horse cannot win every time out, just like humans who have a bad day, so do horses. But those with intelligence and determination will fight to the finish line.

Pops offered, "When I go with my owners kid to buy yearlings, I look for three things. I look for intelligence and serenity in those beautiful eyes. I look at the legs, especially durable, wide hooves. With that foundation the tendons and ligaments line up fair enough. Lastly, I want a strong tail. If I pull on it, and it's stout, there's strength in the hindquarters to win a race. But the will to win is number one kid. Shit, Seabiscuit was a bow-legged runt, but he had the heart of a lion. So, tell me what you think is going on with Rumi?"

Steve had pondered this question himself and had explored the horse's record of no wins over the past two years. In fourteen races she had placed second five times, third three times, and finished the rest in the middle of the pack. "I think she's too nice. She wants to run with the group. She doesn't know how much fun it would be to win the race."

With that, Pops walked away in deep thought.

Chapter 5: Simpatico Souls

THE DAY AFTER HIS THOUGHTFUL ENCOUNTER with Pops, Steven was carefully preparing the water and feeding tub of one dangerous animal named Gal Gloria. She was so aggressive that Steven was the only mucker that the horse had not taken a piece of human flesh from. But Steven had outwitted other people for years, and he used the same logic to handle this animal. He set up a leathery soccer ball on a rope in the far end of the stall. Gloria pounded that thing all day until it resembled a wrinkled orb. On this day Steven barely made it to safety as Gloria preferred a living Steven to a defenseless ball.

Steven admired the raven-coated filly (female horse) from afar. A year older than Rumi Rose, Gal Gloria shared the same mom, Odessa. A legendary multiple stakes winner, Odessa was one of Pops's most successful horses. But their sires (fathers) could not have been more different. Rumi's sire was the relaxed, but race day ready Onyx. Back siders described how Onyx was indifferent to training, but strutted regally on race day, ready to perform. He won six of his first eleven races before a pulled tendon ended his racing career.

Gloria's father was the coal black Obsidian, whose name reflected his mood. Gleeful froth jumped off the horse's whiskers whenever he flipped his jockey, often in the paddock area before a race. Even Pops could not harness Obsidian's considerable talent in the right direction. He was put out to stud at four years of age, after winning four races. Gal Gloria was headed in the same direction, with two victories in her brief career.

Steven was admiring Gloria's midnight coat, so dark it absorbed the sunlight, when he was interrupted by Pops, straw in mouth. "She's named after the owner's wife Gloria." Pops laughed, "He says she's as irascible as his wife. He also owns Rumi, her half sister."

Steven responded, "Was that the well-dressed man I saw you with last week?"

"That's him, David Moriarty from Texas. I'm told he has more oil wells than the Arabs." Pops eyes twinkled, "Pretty clever what you did with the soccer ball. I'm told Gloria hasn't got a taste of you yet."

Steven said sheepishly, "She almost got me today. Look at those eyes. She would like me for dessert."

As if on cue, Gloria removed her head from the feeding tub she was attacking. She snorted and kicked her half-opened stall. Pops laughed, "You're right."

Then, as if talking to himself, Pops continued, "That's what guys like Moriarty don't understand. Horses are prey animals. Mustangs in the wild form packs to protect themselves as they graze. Within that pack you have all different types of personalities. You have dominant and submissive horses, as well as juvenile delinquents, those like Gal Gloria here. They soon learn to accommodate their behavior, or they don't survive."

Pops munched down the twig he just picked up. "You see our horses don't have anyone to protect them. They are all fearful of people, and they have good reason to be. Even Gloria here is operating out of fear. The key is to get them to trust you. And trust requires intelligence. I can look into a colt's (young male horse) eyes and grasp his personality. Sure, a horse needs good bones and genes, but determination which eschews stamina, is what I want."

Pops continued, "Of course, you get incorrigible delinquents, like Gloria here who might never get it. I told Mr. Moriarty to sell her or put her in a claiming race (a race where she can be purchased). But he's afraid of what his wife will say."

Pops appraised Steven and seemed to realize that his young protégé had come to similar conclusions. Steven thoughtfully commented, "I watch how they hold their heads, swish their tails, or perk their ears."

Pops studied him and asked, "What would you do with Gloria here?"

Steven paused, then responded, "Well, if what you said was right about the herd stuff, then I would partner her up with an older, dominating horse. Knock the delinquency out of her."

"Funny kid. I was thinking of something like that myself. I got a six year old filly, Cassandra, that's a hard knocker. She runs in cheap races, but pushes herself to win even over better horses."

Steven then volunteered his conclusions about his favorite horse, "I don't think Rumi knows what she wants. She just goes out to have a good time. If we could squeeze a win out of her, she may come to like it."

Pops chewed on his twig for about a minute. "Okay kid. Rumi's yours to figure out. She's got an allowance race coming up in two months. Let's see if we can't get a win out of her."

Floating on his feet, Steven rushed to Rumi's stall. His mucking days were over – if only temporarily.

The next day, Steven went to work on Rumi. He talked to the horse as he used a curry comb to remove dirt and hair from her reddish-brown coat. "Girl, we got a big chance to make you a star." As if she understood, Rumi nodded her black silk mane, tapping her lustrous coat as Steven proceeded to brush her from head to toe.

Steven consulted with Owen about Rumi's regiment over the next two weeks. She would have three workouts on the track: one a full blown four furlong, the other two mild gallops.

"Owie, have Gal Gloria on the track the day of Rumi's gallop," Steven directed. "I want them to go head to head. Also, I want Ronnie on Rumi for the gallop."

"No can do," said Owen. "He broke his hand the other day. Gloria got another victim."

"Who else we got to ride?"

Owen thought for a minute, "I got a great gal who just came from Somerset Race Track downstate. Her father is a trainer there. She's been around horses her whole life. Her name is Alyssa Conley – goes by Lyssa."

When Steven caught up with Lyssa, her curly locks, a rosier version of Rumi's, he couldn't help but take in her pleasant green eyes, Irish freckled pug nose, and a determined "Don't underestimate me," mouth. Steven immediately liked what he saw. "I want you to run Rumi close to Gloria when you gallop tomorrow," he told her. In fact, so close that Gloria will probably try to bite her half-sister.

Lyssa got it immediately, "So you're saying you are trying to get her angry?"

"Exactly, she's so nice she doesn't know she is supposed to win, and still have fun."

As Steven had predicted, Rumi raced ahead of Gloria, away from the rail. Then detecting the charging hooves behind her, Rumi dallied. A snorting Gloria saw fit to upend Lyssa and attack her half-sibling at the same time. At once sensing the danger, Rumi raced ahead to the finish line. Awaiting her were two large speakers Steven had planted, which began blaring the cheers from a past crowd. In addition, Steven had arranged for the track announcer to feign a broadcast, calling out Rumi's name for the win.

Unbeknown to Steven, Lyssa had arranged for about a hundred of the backside workers to cheer for Rumi at the finish line. Having born the scars of Gloria, they were more than happy to cheer for the sweet Rumi. A prancing Rumi, broad chest and muscular hindquarters bathed in sweat, danced like a rock star responding to her audience.

Steven asked, "Was that your idea, Lyssa, having everyone at the rail?"

Lyssa responded with a wide smile on her tiny jaw, "Yeah. Didn't think they would watch me get killed. That Gloria is crazy."

A smiling Steven agreed, "We will do the same thing next week."

Over coffee the next day, Steven took the opportunity to learn a bit more about this charming jockey, Alyssa Conley.

"My father has always had a small stable of horses down at Arcadia. I was probably in diapers on my first horse. I love riding. But other than from my father, it's hard to get mounts. You know, the girl jockey thing. I came to Templeton to make some money however I could."

"Would you like to ride Rumi next week? I could ask Pops," said a smitten Steven.

Lyssa's green eyes danced. "I would love to," she said as she gave Steven a hug. And with that, Rumi found herself a new jockey for the big day. For the next week Steven served as Rumi's therapist, as he exercised her back and forth along the shed row. "You can do it girl," he told her every day.

Chapter 6: A Star is Born

ON RACE DAY STEVEN WOKE UP at dawn to find a fiery Rumi, as if she was aware of the big day. Steven gently used his curry comb to remove loose hair from her coat. He then carefully brushed her from head to toe. Her reddish-brown coat shined like copper steel. "Remember, Rumi, when Alyssa pulls your mane, it's time to go."

Rumi was to run in a competitive filly only allowance race at 1 and 1/16 miles, the third race of the day. Such a race provided Rumi could not be claimed by another owner. Horses who had not won more than two races at this level were allowed.

Steven surveyed the field, a bit concerned that Rumi was at post one in the nine horse field. *Not good,* he told himself. Steven knew that while the rail is often a good slot - it is the shortest distance to the finish line – it depends on the racing style of the other horses. There were two horses similar to Rumi who liked to go to the lead. Unfortunately, they were in posts two and three, right next to Rumi. If they got out first, they would pin Rumi tight to the rail and prohibit her from taking the lead. At worst she would be trapped in the middle of the pack.

As the first race of the day at Templeton was about to begin, a buzz of excitement filled the air.

Cigar spewing bettors kibbitzed with their racing competition as to why their horses would prevail. Backside workers buzzed to and fro trudging saddles and headgear to the paddock with energetic horses. Trumpets blared to announce the first race as bettors surged to the rails.

As Steven carefully centered the tiny saddle, and fit stirrups for the 110 pound jockey in Race 1, Steven listened to Pops' advice to his top jockey, Henry Romero who was riding Orazio.

"You know he doesn't like crap in his face. Take him wide and keep him away from the crowd. He has one good lick in him – at the 5/8's pole (a third of a mile to the finish line) let him make his move."

Henry nodded and laughed as Steven led horse and jockey to the starting gate. *Pops makes it sound so easy.*

As the gates opened, Henry maneuvered his stallion Orazio just off the pace, almost isolated into the Clubhouse turn. Pops liked that the pace was moderate – 49 seconds for the half mile – and watched as Henry urged Orazio to engage the three horses in front of him. At the 5/8 pole instructed location, Henry engaged the remaining two leaders, their legs churning, but their thundering hooves slowly devoid of past propulsion.

Henry leaned into Orazio, feeling the surge of energy as horse and jockey became one, to chase the only horse now in front of him, the number six horse Angelo's Ashes, the betting favorite, just two lengths ahead. "Come on boy," Henry whispers, face tight on Orazio's mane. As the two horses run neck and neck, Henry cannot hear the sea of excitement around him; there is only silence. He feels the muscles exploding underneath him. Determination controls Henry's senses as he inches eye to eye with the frontrunner. "I got him." Henry immediately knows he has Orazio's nose in front of Angelo's Ashes. His magic ride has ended in less than two minutes, and he raises his arms in victory!

Pops gives Steven the mildest of hugs as he races out to the winner's circle to welcome Orazio. Steven is not as gleeful because Race 2 will soon begin, and Alyssa Conley is nowhere in sight. Steven had convinced Pops to choose Alyssa over Henry to ride Rumi, and he was worried. "Pops will never let me train another horse," he said to himself. Just then he noticed a visibly upset Alyssa.

"Where the hell have you been?"

"I'm sorry Stevie. My dad had a problem, so I had to go home."

"Whatever," muttered an irritated Steven as they raced to Rumi's stall.

When they reached the stall, Steven once again advised Alyssa. "Lyss you got lots of speed right beside you. Try to get the lead and if not, don't get into a speed dual. Let them fight it out and pick them off. If Rumi doesn't get the lead, drop her down to the fence and wait. Remember, no whip. When you want her to run, tug hard on her mane."

Lyssa understood that Rumi always liked to run on the lead, and the horse might fight her to chase the pace. She turned to Steven, and apologized again, "I really am sorry about today, Stevie."

Steven just waved her off. “She’s ready. Just let her win.”

The starting gates clanged open and Lyssa almost got pinched out of the saddle. Her leg was crushed by the horseflesh next to her. Horse three had spun left into gate 2, which cascaded all three horses pinballing all over the track. Lyssa found herself going east and west for twenty yards, while her competitors straightened out to the lead. Getting control of a startled Rumi, Lyssa found herself dead last, the next horse five lengths ahead.

Even Rumi sensed she was in unchartered territory, as she loved to run with the pack. Without encouragement, Rumi picked up her speed, running the half mile in a moderate 49 1/5 seconds. Soon Rumi was in her favorite place – happily running with her equine mates. At the quarter pole Lyssa told herself, “It’s now or never for this girl.” She firmly tugged on Rumi’s mane. Lyssa felt a surge of tightened power beneath her as a new Rumi left her friends behind. Arching into the final turn, Rumi seemed to glide over the track surface, like a bolt of electricity. Lyssa marveled at the passing scenery of horseflesh coming into and then behind her vision.

At the finish line, a moment of complete silence, and then a burst of cheers from the fans. They had witnessed a last to first finish quarter mile race in an amazing 22 seconds.

The guest on this incredible athlete, Lyssa is nearly drained of energy. She can barely wrap her arms around the heaving horseflesh. Not so Rumi… Chest heaving, sweat turning her coat blood red, she prances in front of the adoring fans. Her ears perked high as if hearing her praises. "So this is what winning is all about!"

Steven is the first to congratulate both athletes, as Lyssa jumped from the saddle into Steven's arms. "She's incredible, Stevie." Steven caresses Rumi's muzzle, her whiskers frothing saliva on Steven's face.

Pops puts a paternal hand on Steven's shoulder. "Congratulations kid, you figured her out. Why don't you hot walk Rumi. I'll get Owie to help me in the next race."

"Walking hots" is a crucial step in the recovery of the equine's arduous run. This cooling down process by "hot walking" in the backside allows the horses' muscles to slowly relax. This task is normally done by stable hands, but Steven is honored to walk his protégé round and round the backside. For Steven and Rumi it resembles a therapy session, as other attendants watch and shake their heads. "They seem to speak a different language," said a long time stable hand, observing trainer and horse engage one another.

Following Rumi's win, Steven went back to work helping Pops in the five final races. Race 7 was marred by the obstinate Gal Gloria, who never made it out of the starting gate. She attacked the valet who was attempting to strap the girth around her belly. She then refused to get into the starting gate by assaulting the six starters who tried to guide her in. The track veterinarian disqualified her from the race. Pops had one more winner in the final

Race 9, but Steven performed his myriad of tasks stoically. His mind was elsewhere.

Why had Alyssa been late for the race? More importantly, was her jump into his arms from Rumi something more personal? Steven had to admit he had a different kind of feeling for Lyssa than he had ever experienced. Past girlfriends were all about sex. Normally, when he had sex with them he thought less of them. He didn't dwell on why. Just move on to the next girl that catches his eye.

But Lyssa was different. He wondered if she had a boyfriend. His thoughts, *What does she think about me?* were unique for Steven. He knew one thing – nothing would stop him from being a successful trainer. And he would enjoy all the money and fame that it would bring. He would show the world that he, Steven Ricci, was no shmuck. *But where did this girl jockey fit into his plans?*

Following the races Steven found Lyssa at the backside canteen, fondling a beer. She did not appear to be enjoying her first victory at Templeton. "How are you doing Lyssa?"

The thrill of riding Rumi looked to be a distant past in those tear filled eyes. "I wanted to explain why I was late Stevie." Averting eye contact Lyssa continued, "I wasn't with my father. I have been dating Nicky Bianco, who rides down in Arcadia. We have known each other for about a year. He started exercising horses for my father and then became his top jockey. He's a big deal down there now, the winningest jockey. He may be coming up here to work for Talbert Farms."

When he heard the name Nicky Bianco, Steven's face reddened as he recalled their unlawful past, but he remained silent.

"Anyway," Lyssa continued, "For some reason Nicky did not want me to ride Rumi. He would not give me a reason. I told him, Nicky, this is my big chance to ride at Templeton. He just said no, and if I ride, we are broken up." She sobbed, "I didn't know what to do. I went back and forth. I even got in my car early yesterday but drove back. I still have strong feelings for him. I'm really mixed up. That's why I was late."

Steven absorbed this in the way a selfish person would. "He couldn't love you Lyssa. I wouldn't do that to someone. You are still Rumi's jockey if you want to ride her."

With that Steven left Alyssa with her beer. He had to brush Rumi and make her bed of hay extra snug. He also had to figure out a way into Lyssa's heart. Or was it his desire to get revenge on Nicky Bianco?

Chapter 7: Steven's Strategic Moves

STEVEN HAD 24 HOURS to develop a duel strategy – to win Alyssa's heart and to figure out Gal Gloria's dogged behavior. Overnight he had convinced himself that the angelic Lyssa deserved him. Following Rumi's victory, Pops sent him a blunt message, "Get Gal Gloria to the Winner's Circle."

But of more immediate importance was to win Alyssa's heart. The fact that she dated Nicky Bianco in the first place only sweetened his attraction to her. "I'll show him," filled his smug mindset. He began to calculate a strategy to win her heart.

In the next few days, happy that the ambivalent Alyssa had not returned to Arcadia, Steven prepared Rumi for her workouts. Pops had taught him that like all athletes, horses need a couple of days to soothe those thick muscles. After that, back to a regiment of hard work. Too stagnant, and the tight belly pouring into the hind quarters softens like butter.

As Alyssa approached, Steven said, "Just a light workout today, Lyssa.

A subdued Lyssa replied, "Sure thing Stevie." She was the only person that ever called him that.

Following the workout Steven tightened his grip on the rope shank leading Rumi to her paddock with Alyssa astride.

"How about we get a coffee at the canteen," he suggested. Soon Steven and Alyssa were greeted by a bellowing Southern voice, "Grits for the big trainer?" Sheila, the engaging cook could hardly hold back, "I hear Pops is grooming you to take over his herd."

"Pops has forgotten more than I know," said a smiling Steven. But Steven was aware that he was being measured on the backside more seriously. Still only 21 years old, Steven was now called Mr. Ricci by some of the grooms who were much older than he was. As another measure of respect, Pops had taught Steven how to add his special nutrients and vitamins to the horses' barley and oats. Even Mr. Moriarty, the largest horse owner at Templeton and Pops's benefactor paid Steven a compliment. "Good job with Rumi kid. Keep it up." With all this praise Steven sensed he should adopt a modest façade.

More taps on the back followed as Steven picked an isolated picnic table to unveil his plan with Alyssa. "I want to talk to you about Nicky Bianco. I know him. He's from Arcadia where I grew up. He's a bit older than me, and I got into some trouble with him. You see, we both didn't have fathers and maybe that's why we connected."

But his lying blue eyes moistened as he said with all the sincerity he could muster, "He got me into robbing houses with some older kids. That's why I had to leave Arcadia. He got arrested. I know that."

To add effect, Steven pulled out an article from the Arcadia Telegram, which named Nicky as one of those arrested. "I just want you to know what kind of person he is."

"I can't believe it," said Alyssa, as she fingered the crumpled newspaper article. "He seems so nice. Do you think that's why he didn't want me to ride Rumi?"

Steven knew better than to answer. Instead, he pulled his hands from his coffee and put them on hers. "I think we should be together." He laughed, "You, me and Rumi make a great team."

Alyssa smiled. She did not remove her hands from Steven's.

Then he shrewdly brought Pops into the equation, commenting on how Pops had been so excited about Steven's success with Rumi. Steven knew that the impressionable Lyssa loved Pops like a kindly grandfather. She had told him often, "My father idolized Pops. He learned everything from him."

After a few moments, Alyssa said, "Do you know that Pops taught Nicky everything about being a jockey?"

"Yeah I heard."

Steven's thoughts went to the stories he had heard from Owie, and the day when Owie had eyed him warily as he warned, "I hope you don't fuck Pops like Nicky did." He knew from Owie that Nicky was an old "mucker" who had started just like him. This was Steven's chance to tell Alyssa what he knew about Nicky, and turn her against him.

"Lyssa, Owie told me that Pops taught Nicky how to ride. And Nicky learned well. You know he's up for the top apprentice jockey award in the country. Pops planned for Nicky to be his top rider when he retired. But Nicky left. He didn't care about Pops. And now he's going to sign with Caldwell Farms, Pops's biggest competitor. He screwed Pops." Then, with his most heartfelt gaze into Alyssa's eyes, Steven said, "I would never betray Pops."

To this last bit of news Alyssa's soft eyes grew flinty. "I can't believe Nicky would repay Pops like that."

And with this engineered conversation, Steven wooed himself into Alyssa's heart. Over the next year jockey and trainer grew inseparable, on and off the racetrack.

During the next year Lyssa rode Rumi to three more victories - one a Grade 3 race with a purse of $250,000. Lyssa's tidy 10% of that purse combined with Steven's earnings as Pops's top assistant allowed the couple to buy a modest home near Templeton.

Trainer and Jockey also collaborated to penetrate the dangerous psyche of Rumi's half-sister, Gal Gloria. Alyssa suggested that they get a dog for her, "I hear an animal can soften the horses up."

Steven thought about the white, brown-eyed mongrel that had been tailing him lately. The dog was an orphan, who appeared at Templeton one day. He told Alyssa, "Let's bring Fluffy into Gloria's stall. The worst she can do is kill her!"

Alyssa rolled her eyes, and then seemed to regret her own idea about a dog in the stall. "You'd better keep that dog safe."

Fortunately, Gloria and Fluffy took to each other like two lost souls who had finally found one another. Rather than bite the mongrel, Gloria licked Fluffy's soft fur. Horse and dog were found dreaming in their separate hay beds when Steven awoke them at 5 a.m. each day.

Gal Gloria's improved psyche led the relaxed filly to win two of her four next races. Steven observed that she was a "need to lead horse." If she got a quick lead by herself, she would win. Unlike Rumi however, when Gloria felt competition she often faded to second or third.

As Steven's fingerprints became more noticeable to trackside observers, Steven received more than a nod from the horses' owner, David Moriarty. Always impeccably dressed in pinstripe suits and clean oxford shoes that seemed averse to mud, Mr. Moriarty was an odd presence in "shed row". Tall and bespeckled with skin the color of a gray colt, he would seem more comfortable buying and selling oil companies, which in fact, he did. Steven imagined him in knickers and high socks attending privileged schools as a child. He spoke in a high-pitched voice that combined a Kentucky twang with a Brahmin east coast affect, pronouncing "again" as "agane."

"That man never had to worry about money a day in his life," thought Steven the first time he saw Mr. Moriarty.

But even Steven was amazed at how those pasty aristocratic features came alive when Mr. Moriarty talked about one of his horses. One day, while Steven and Alyssa were bathing Rumi, Mr. Moriarty walked by. He was in deep thought, both hands in the pockets of his banker suit, when he suddenly stopped in mid-step.

"You are Steven and Lyssa, right. Pops speaks highly of you both."

Taken aback by the strange diction, Steven and Alyssa looked at each other. "I'm David Moriarty, the owner. And you are Rumi's trainer and jockey."

"Yes sir," the couple finally blurted out.

"Well, you are both doing a great job. Let's keep it up."

With that he walked away, his pristine suit soon out of sight. Finally, Alyssa spoke, "Strange guy huh."

Steven laughed, "Yeah, strange, but rich. At least he knows our names."

Shortly after this encounter with Mr. Moriarty, Steven and Alyssa received another visit from Gloria's owner. This time the real Gloria, Mr. Moriarty's young wife was with him. She was smartly attired, with high heels not suitable for the muddy backside. She held out her long tapered red fingernailed hand, adorned with several sparkling diamond rings, as if she half expected Steven to kiss it.

"She looks like a real bitch," thought Steven, as he shook her hand. Steven figured there was at least a twenty-year age gap between the distinguished couple.

"I guess I should thank you for attempting to make Gloria a winner," she laughed. "After all, she is giving me a bad name."

Steven could not assess the comments' purpose, since Gloria's eyes were hidden behind oversized gold sunglasses. With that, the princess wife, showcasing her trim figure, sashayed out of the mud. "Come on David, let's get some lunch."

"One second honey," her husband said in the strange diction Steven now understood. The older man approached Steven and asked, "What do you think about running two-year-olds in races?" Steven knew the purpose of this question, and hesitated. His answer might change his racing life.

Chapter 8: Changes in the Templeton Air

FOR THE QUESTION POSED BY MR. MORIARTY represented a philosophical breach that distinguished Steven Ricci and Pops. More than once Pops had emphasized to Steven that horseracing is all about the horse.

"These horses are born to run, Steven. That is why God has blessed them with chest and hindquarters that propel those skinny legs so fast. Our job is to harness that love into a sport made by humans. Our job is to take care of them, my friend, since the bettors and definitely the owners don't give a shit about them."

And up until that point Steven had deviated from his past history of using others for his own benefit. He genuinely loved these beautiful animals that simultaneously conveyed power and grace. Unlike people, these animals touched something in him that not even Alyssa could match, although she came the closest.

But Mr. Moriarty's question was something that had lingered in Steven's young mind for a bit. Pops was content to be one of the top trainers in the country but remain mostly unnoticed. And Steven knew that Pops had tutored him so carefully because Pops saw the love in Steven's eyes for the animals. But this confederacy only went so far.

Steven wanted to be noticed and become rich. He had seen Mr. Moriarty and his cronies posing with their horses at pre- and post-race celebrations. Other than appearing in the winner's circle – a slight smile on Pops's face directed at the horse – the older trainer would disappear into his hay filled "office", content to celebrate with his horses.

Beyond his desire to be celebrated, Steven noticed some small things about Pops's approach that needled him. More than once Pops had scratched a horse because as he said, "The horse just wasn't right." This, despite the veterinarian's diagnosis that the horse was fine to run. Once Pops even scratched Mr. Moriarty's horse Sir Regal, just before the top race, the Templeton Million, because Pops suspected laminitis in the horse (an inflammation of the hoof wall.) Pops scratched (eliminated from the race) Sir Regal despite Mr. Moriarty's top vet insisting that the hoof was not "hot." The vet made this decision after sliding his fingers below the fetlock to satisfactorily measure the digital pulse of the foot.

But all Pops would say was, "He's not running," as an exasperated Mr. Moriarty commented out of earshot, "I have to get myself another trainer!" However, Mr. Moriarty didn't fire Pops because one week later, even the vet shook his head, when Sir Regal had an inflamed hoof.

Steven, however, silently commiserated with Mr. Moriarty. "It was a million-dollar race," Steven thought. "I would have run Sir Regal with a slight inflammation. It wasn't going to kill him."

It was Pops' s position on racing two-year-old thoroughbreds that separated him from almost any other trainer in the country. The horse world celebrates all racing horses birthdays on January first of the calendar year. This is done for racing efficiency. So a horse born in January or December in one calendar year turns two after being a yearling at one. Most trainers begin to run their horses at two years of age, against similar aged horses. The horses are most often started with short distances of four to five furlongs. (In a horse race a mile is equivalent to eight furlongs.)

Despite the opinion of the horse racing world, that it is safe to race horses at two years of age, Pops thought otherwise. Sponging down a horse one day while Pops puffed on his pipe, Steven asked him why Pops thought that way.

Pops answered, "Think of a horse's legs like your own, Kid. There's the thigh, knee and ankle, but a hoof instead of a foot. Horses have only one toe underneath that hoof. The wall and tissue in that hoof form a protective shell, that only develop with the horse's maturity. You got bad feet, and the rest of the leg goes to pot. I won with horses that had bowed legs, but never one with bad hooves. Let those hooves get a good blood supply, and the horse can run until he's ten years old."

But as Mr. Moriarty watched other owners getting rich with their two year olds, he grew frustrated. He confronted his trainer, "Pops, I don't need my horses to run until they're ten. I need them to run now."

The unfazed gerbil like face, his head adorned with his beret responded, "Well maybe you should get yourself one of those fancy trainers."

Steven wordlessly watched these interactions.

In the end Mr. Moriarty always bit his tongue, unlike he did with his oil-world competitors. "You're crazy Pops." But the next day he would appear at the stable to take Pops to the annual yearling sales. For along with Pops's unrivaled ability to train horses, he also had a sixth sense as to which horses Mr. Moriarity should add to his stable.

Most horse owners appeared with youthful buyer agents, who dressed like bankers and had fancy equipment to measure the young horses' hearts and lungs. The nebbish buyers looked aghast as Pops, wearing stained pants, would stare into the horses' eyes, pull on their tails, and eye-ball their hooves.

"Take this one," was all Pops would say, just as he did with Templeton's new star, Rumi Rose.

The observant and shrewd Steven understood all these dynamics in the Pops-Mr. Moriarty relationship. *Not now,* Steven told himself, as Mr. Moriarty waited expectantly for his answer to the two year old age racing question.

Steven slowly nodded his head as he responded, "I agree with Pops. You might get a short-term gain for long term failure Mr. Moriarty."

Mr. Moriarty's eyes absorbed Steven as the young man responded – as if measuring Steven's true feelings. "Okay, Steven. Let's get Gloria out there soon, okay."

"Sure boss," said Steven, unsure if he had passed Mr. Moriarty's test.

But Steven hid his true feelings for the next two years. He was acknowledged by the Templeton staff and other horsemen as the successor to Pops. Pops would give praise to Steven the way he summed up his horses, "The kid got good eyes." And by the actions he displayed Pops demonstrated his confidence in Steven's judgement. Pops allowed Steven to monitor the conditions of eligibility for Mr. Moriarty's stable, and so Steven could enroll the horses in more demanding stakes races as the young protegee saw fit.

Pops brought Steven to the woods and showed him the various mushrooms and plants he added to the horses' feeds. Pops had never shared that knowledge even with his trusted foreman Owie. And it was Pops who sponsored Steven's trainer application in the state of Kentucky. The night Steven received his trainer's license Pops took the new trainer, Lyssa, and Owie out to his favorite Templeton restaurant, "Beavers." It was the only time Templeton folks saw Pops drink wine, as he proposed a toast to Steven's success.

It was soon after getting his own license that Steven deviated from Pops's mantra about horse safety. A colleague of Pops, a small time trainer, Chris Valente, came to Steven one day following another loss. His horse, Mr. McConaghy, was running in a small claiming race that day. Chris's five horse stable had only two wins in thirty attempts for the meet. Pops was out of town one Saturday when Chris approached Steven as he watched a farrier nail new horseshoes on Rumi Rose.

"Can I talk to you Steven?"

"Sure. What's up? Hope you can get a win today."

"Mr. McConaghy has been training well."

With that, a nervous Chris looked around and lowering his voice said, "Can I talk to you alone."

Turning to the farrier, Steven said, "Ed, I'll be right back." Nails protruding from his mouth prompted only a nod of the head.

When they were out of Ed's hearing, Chris began, "Steven, you know my jockey Rafael has not had a win all year. His kid is in the hospital for some sort of heart issue. The other jockeys want to help him out and get him a winner's purse. They are going to go wide in the stretch and let Mr. McConaghy win."

Steven immediately understood Chris was asking for Steven's horse David's Delight to lose on purpose. Chicanery like this on a horse track can lead to injury – to both human and horse.

Steven was incredulous. He knew funny business went on in the sport. Some trainers used illegal medications or electric buzzers to stimulate the horses, but this was different. Getting all the jockeys on board was serious business. Reading Steven's face, Chris said, "It's for a good cause, Steven. I'm even giving my share of the purse to Rafael."

"Is Nicky on board with this?" Steven asked. Nicky was the infamous Nicky Bianco who was now the top jockey at Templeton. Steven's worries about Nicky Bianco's appearance had evaporated from the day he came to Templeton a year ago. He had shaken Steven's hand, neither man betraying their history with one another. As for Alyssa, Nicky was dating owner Jim Caldwell's daughter and seemed content to move on romantically. In fact, in the jockeys' room pre- and post-race, Nicky was protective of his former girlfriend when the guys teased her saying, "Lyss you wouldn't be here if not for Steven."

Nicky would quickly respond with, "Shut up you guys." She's a better jockey than any of you."

To Steven's question about Nicky being on board Chris answered, "It was Nicky's idea. He's riding the favorite Odessa, and he's going to burn him up fast. Can you get Lyssa on board with David's Delight? The other jockeys are going wide in the final turn to let Mr. McConaghy come up the rail."

Steven debated internally. He knew Pops would never cheat in a race, even for a good cause. But he said he would talk to Lyssa.

"I don't like it Stevie. I feel uncomfortable," was Alyssa's expected response.

"Look, Rafael's kid might die if he doesn't get this operation," was Steven's false argument that acquiesced his partner.

Watching the eight horse field in the paddock, Steven realized the conspiracy had taken no chances for Mr. McConaghy's win. He observed that three of the horses must have had salty breakfasts. They looked bloated and must have consumed gallons of water prior to the race.

Odessa, however, looked live- strutting and snorting in the paddock as if saying to the other horses, "You guys got no chance." Steven thought to himself, *Nicky is going to have a tough time losing this race.*

A chronic loser, Mr. McConaghy, with two victories in his career, had not won in over a year. His odds reflected that record. With five minutes to post his odds were 40 to 1. He was fit, however, and usually ran mid-pack until the final turn when he faded to his usual fourth or fifth.

Alyssa got her instructions before the race, "Take Delight out unusually fast Lyssa, maybe 44 seconds for the half mile. Then he will have little left in the tank when he goes up the rail."

And that is how the race developed. Nicky took the normally slow-moving Odessa out to an insane 21 seconds in the first quarter mile. From the rail, Steven thought, *No way can Odessa hold that lead.* Mr. McConaghy was 14 lengths behind Odessa and seven lengths behind the next closest horse at the half mile.

And then it happened. As if a fireman's ladder pushed six horses outside, the jockeys, in unison, ushered their horses wide. A surprised Mr. McConaghy accepted the invitation and ran hard to the rail. As Odessa's exhausted tongue hung from her mouth, Nicky released the reins to no avail. Odessa was going to win on her will alone. Two lengths from the finish line and a length ahead of Mr. McConaghy, Nicky had a decision to make. Acting like a Western movie actor, who had been bucked from his horse, he leapt from Odessa.

Mr. McConaghy had his third career victory, as Rafael made the Sign of the Cross once he passed the finish line. As he watched the winning horse strut to the finish line, Steven sensed that even Mr. McConaghy was surprised by his success.

Chapter 9: Surprises in the Air

FOLLOWING MR. MCCONAGHY'S surprising win, Steven ran into Nicky as he marched into the racing steward's office. Nicky would have to satisfactorily explain his actions at the end of the race. However, having a good reputation, and being the winningest jockey at Templeton, he would be given plenty of slack by the racing officials. And having Mr. Caldwell, the owner of the largest car dealerships in the state of Kentucky as your boss, would also help.

"I knew you would have trouble with Odessa. She would run with a broken leg," commented Steven.

Nicky laughed, "She is amazing, but it was the right thing to do."

Steven walked away from that brief encounter perplexed. Nicky was acting so unlike Steven would have acted if someone had stolen his girl. He thought, *I would never forgive someone for screwing me.* But Nicky seemed so sincere and had done the right thing for poor Rafael. Tossing this over in his mind Steven thought, *I would never have suggested the idea of helping someone like Raphael. And about how Nicky has been treating me. Not only did I rat him out to the police, but I stole his girl."*

Steven kept thinking about Nicky's actions. When Alyssa told him how protective Nicky was of her in the jockey room, Steve grew more obsessed. *Was Nicky hatching a plan for retribution, or did he really not care? Nicky certainly made the right call dating Mr. Caldwell's daughter Tiffany.* The couple had appeared on every celebrity column in the Templeton newspapers. And Steven was a bit jealous to see the tuxedoed Nicky win the Templeton "Jockey of the Year" award, the blonde, doe-faced Tiffany looking on in admiration.

Although Steven really cared for Alyssa, she would never introduce him into the glamorous world that Tiffany had been born into. Down deep Steven could only half-admit to himself that he wished he could find a "Tiffany." Unfortunately, Mr. Moriarty had no daughters.

It was soon after the Mr. Moriarty victory that Steven received a surprise. Rumi Rose had another sweet victory. It was her third victory of the year, occurring in a demanding grade 3 race. She led wire to wire in the $200,000 race. Mr. Moriarty insisted on Steven and Alyssa joining him at the elite jockey club banquet later that night.

Not even the owner of a tuxedo, Steven felt somewhat uncomfortable as he surveyed the crowd of elite owners and guests at this festive venue. Ornate chandeliers seemed to accentuate the diamonds of statuesque ladies wearing long sequenced gowns, carrying fancy cocktails, and hanging on the arms of formally dressed gentlemen. A ten piece band played quietly in the background, allowing the buzzing guests to chatter, laugh, and jealously eyeball one another.

Alyssa tightened her grip on Steven's arm as she too sensed that people could see the couple were not one of them. However, unlike Alyssa, Steven grew relaxed quickly.

So this is how it feels.

He could not help but notice that a crowd of these "buzzers' were flying around one particular couple. Straining to gaze through the human maze, Steven identified the celebrity couple – a tanned Nicky Bianco, and his companion, Tiffany, her blonde hair crowned with a diamond tiara.

Just then a serious Mr. Moriarty grabbed the couple by the arms. "Glad you both could make it." Also looking at the commotion the young couple on the other side of the room was causing, Mr. Moriarty commented, "I heard they just got engaged." He then ushered Steven and Alyssa over to his table where his wife was sitting. "Gloria, look who I just found."

Mr. Moriarty's words interrupted Steven's envious thoughts, *That Nicky is a lucky bastard.*

"Gloria, you remember Steven and Lyssa?"

"Of course," said the bored looking forty something young woman. Her bouffant raven hair was piled high on her head, revealing sparkling diamond earrings that Steven estimated were five carrots. Gloria immediately asked about her equine namesake. "How is Gal Gloria doing?"

"Oh, we are giving her a rest right now. She should be running in a couple of months. But her attitude is like day and night as to what it was, Pops got her figured out."

Although Alyssa sat between Steven and Gloria, the sophisticate addressed only Steven. "I think you are being modest young man," she smiled. "They tell me Pops is ready to retire."

"I don't think he will ever retire," interrupted Alyssa, seeking to be part of the conversation.

Gloria continued to look directly at Steven, "Are you only successful with female horses?"

Pretending to ignore the provocative question, Steven put his arm around Alyssa. "Don't forget Lyssa will ride Gal Gloria to all her victories."

After an awkward silence, Steven grabbed Alyssa's arm and said, "Let's dance."

So they took to the dance floor. But neither as nimble away from the horse track, they stepped on each other's toes as they danced in a small circle.

Alyssa was first to comment, "I hate it here Steven. Let's get out of here and grab a beer at the backside. She studied Steven to garner his reaction.

But Steven was ignoring her gaze and caressing the atmosphere with his eyes. "It's not so bad."

Alyssa pulled him closer, "Tell me you'll never leave me Steven."

"Sure," he answered staring briefly into her eyes, and then returning his gaze to the liquor induced buzz around him.

Just then Mr. Moriarty grabbed the couple again, sweeping them through the dancing flesh of all sizes. Soon they were at the Caldwell table. "Jim, this is Pops's top assistant, Steven Ricci."

This energetic former car salesman stood tall and put a ferocious grasp on Steven's hand. "I've heard a lot about you, young man."

Steven immediately sensed the two different worlds of Mr. Moriarty and Mr. Caldwell. Jim Caldwell spoke like someone from Arcadia, someone who was on a fast mission to make money and flaunt it – someone like himself. This was the difference between "old" and "new" money.

Looking at this Adonis-like fast talking owner, Steven could picture this aggressive man succeeding in the car business on energy alone. Steven instantly admired him.

Mr. Moriarty continued the introductions, "And this is Steven's girlfriend Alyssa Conley, also one of our jockeys."

After nodding at Alyssa, Mr. Caldwell smiled at the beautiful, golden-haired women beside him, "This is my wife Denise, and our daughter Tiffany."

Steven quickly recognized that Denise was Tiffany, only twenty-five years older. He envisioned that Denise was probably the popular cheerleader who won a young Caldwell's heart. Tiffany sat next to her sister-like mother.

"And I believe you know Nicky Bianco. He tells me you both came from Arcadia."

With that Nicky came over to give a warm hug to Steven and Alyssa. "Yes, we go way back," said Nicky.

Mr. Moriarty got down to business, "Well Jim, I want you to know that I'm thinking of running Rumi in the Templeton Million in the spring."

"Really?" responded a surprised Jim. "You know a filly has never won the Templeton. She'll be running against only males."

"I know, I know," said David Moriarty, "but this girl's a bit different."

Jim's ego revealed itself, "I don't think anyone in the country can beat Alex the Great. If you want a side wager, just name the price David."

Like a dignified patrician, David simply smiled and said, "That might be fun."

After listening to this conversation, Steven was deeply worried. Sure, Rumi was a good, very good filly, but Alex the Great was a multiple Grade 1 winner. He had won a Triple Crown race and had never lost a race at Templeton. In addition, very few females ever beat male horses, particularly in Grade 1 horse races. "Have you discussed this with Pops?" said a fretful Steven.

"Leave Pops to me," responded Mr. Moriarty.

Later that night, Steven and Alyssa lay in each other's arms discussing the events of that evening.

"Lyss, you know this could be a big chance for us. If Rumi ever wins, both of us would be famous."

"I don't think I can ride Rumi, Stevie." Alyssa turned and straddled Steven's prone, naked body. Looking deeply into Steven's eyes, she whispered, "We are having a baby." She kissed him deeply.

His reaction was not what she expected. Pushing her off him, Steven stumbled out of the bed. "How did this happen?"

Taken aback Alyssa responded, "Steven you know I wasn't on the pill. What did you expect would happen?"

"But I wasn't expecting…I don't know if it's the right time."

"There might never be a right time," murmured Alyssa.

Growing quiet, Steven accepted the invitation to join Alyssa on the bed. Alyssa became adamant, "I am not going to have an abortion, Steven. I know that's what you're thinking."

"But, but…"

"Shh…" Alyssa put her finger to Steven's mouth, "You're going to be a father, and I think you will be a great one. Remember, you never had the gift of a father, Stevie. Besides, you will need a better jockey than me for Rumi. I'm not ready for the Templeton. If I am honest, I was happiest as an exercise rider when I could have fun with the horses."

And with that, the debate was over. Steven Ricci would experience fatherhood whether he wanted to or not.

Chapter 10: The Wedding

THE FOLLOWING MORNING AT FIRST LIGHT, the backside at Templeton awoke with its normal frenzy. The pampered horses were being washed, fed, and brushed as workers attended to the horses' every need. All this activity made the stoic Pops all the more noticeable as he sat in his "office."

Approaching the older man, Steven said, "You missed a great party last night Pops. I even met Mr. Caldwell. He seemed like a nice guy."

Ignoring the comment, Pops got right to the point, "I don't like Rumi running against the boys, especially Alex the Great. He's the best horse I've seen in a long time."

"Pops, the worst that can happen is Rumi loses. But maybe she wins."

"So you're on board with Rumi running in the race?" Pops blue eyes riveted on Steven's face.

"Well," responded Steven, "Mr. Moriarty just told me about it last night, but I think Rumi is really starting to get it. And we've got six months before the Templeton, Pops, why don't we see how she trains."

"You might be right Steven. But she might have too much heart."

"What do you mean, too much heart?" asked Steven.

Pops did not respond.

"Anyway, I do have good news Pops. Lyssa is pregnant, and we are going to get married as soon as we can."

Hearing that news, the concern left Pops's face. "That's great Steven. She is a wonderful girl. Her dad and I go way back. He must be thrilled. You're a lucky guy Steven. She'll make a great mother."

"But I think I lost a good jockey," said a smiling Steven. With that, Steven and Pops embraced.

Despite David Moriarty's attempts to have the couple married at Templeton's elite jockey club, Alyssa nixed that idea. She told Steven, "I don't want that fancy place. These are the people I care about, the muckers and riders we work with every day.

Plans for the special day were soon underway. Who knew that besides cooking a superb chicken fried steak, Shelia had the skills of a 5th Avenue interior decorator. In a matter of two weeks, she turned farriers and hot walkers into first rate carpenters and painters. Muddy floor tiles were replaced by a stylish gray rug, a gift from a local carpet store owner who also owned horses. Mr. Moriarty donated curtains from one of his many homes under renovation. Sheila had caressed multiple layers of sheers and curtains to dramatic effect. Tired windows and walls were then covered with a wave of fabric ripples cascading from ceiling to floor. The best white furniture from the local Rent-A-Center was accentuated by special floodlights.

Sheila, in Hitchcockian fashion belted out orders. "Shine these lights on the head table. We want those lights on the dance floor and away from the mice in the corners."

Lastly, she orchestrated a pig-roast paint party to paint the outside of the canteen. The men and women of the backside picked up paint brushes instead of rakes and did the job. The exterior was painted a pretty baby blue, Alyssa's favorite color, to spruce up the drab shed row.

On the special day the workers' calloused hands were scrubbed clean, and they stood tall in their best jeans and polished boots. It was as if the workers were in the Ritz-Carlton, a Ritz they helped create. Years later the same workers would speak in awe of that special day.

Steven and Alyssa were married at Templeton's famous finish line. Alyssa's father Bill Conley and Pops served as best men. Jockey Henry Romero got permission to perform the ceremony. He sat fittingly on Rumi Rose, as other ponies coalesced around the horse folks. The only guest in a suit and tie was Mr. Moriarty. A smiling Nicky Bianco arrived with Tiffany Caldwell, who did look a bit out of place as her diamond bracelet and necklace got "Look at that" scowls from the female jockeys.

At the conclusion of the ceremony Alyssa and Steven kissed as a cascade of cowboy hats filled the air.

Next the wedding revelers headed to the luminous canteen, where a Western hoedown filled the night. Backside workers with previously unknown guitar skills performed with a talented country western quartet chosen by Mr. Moriarty. Sheila prepared a country style buffet – fried chicken, barbeque ribs, and rich apple pie. Guests square danced around the happy couple. Alyssa was dazzling in her white laced gown accentuated by sparkling sequins and a long lace train and her new husband was equally handsome in his baby blue tux, stiff white shirt, black cummerbund and bow tie.

The couple were soon enjoying the spirited party. A coatless Steven kicked up his legs as he locked arms with a group of his male coworkers in a long line. Not to be outdone, another line of the women workers matched high kicks with the men. Alyssa had to carefully lift her long train to enjoy her kicks.

At some point Steven had a chance to slow dance with his mother, Carole. Since his departure from her home four years earlier, the two had adopted a cool relationship. Steven sensed that given the trouble he had caused her, she was happy to be distanced from him. When he first revealed he was working at Templeton, she seemed relieved. Six months later, at Thanksgiving, she gave him another reason to stay away. She introduced him to her boyfriend, a ruddy faced fireman from Arcadia, named Paul "Duck" Duckman. Duck was a local guy who liked to brag about his high school touchdowns in between sucking down beers. Duck also did himself no favors in his first meeting with Steven when he mentioned Steven's past delinquency.

I heard you were a pretty bad kid," said Duck. "Good you got out of Arcadia Steven. Those guys you hung with are all in jail."

Steven figured Duck's police softball buddies had told him about Steven's past. When his mother married Duck a year ago, Steven did not go to the wedding as he had races to attend to.

Carole surprised her son as they slow danced at his wedding. She looked up at him, smiled and said, "Your dad would be so proud of you."

Carole's comment was a surprise to Steven because his father had been a continued invisible presence in their home. Steven rarely asked about him and Carole completed the invisibility by hardly ever bringing up his name. The picture of a Marine in uniform that a young Steven admired no longer collected dust in the living room.

Mother and son continued to dance in silence until at one point Carole looked over to a couple snuggling in the dark corner of the canteen. Her attention drawn to the woman's sparkling necklace, Carole pursed her lips and whispered, "Is that Nicky Bianco from Arcadia?"

"Yeah Mom, that's him. He's a top jockey here."

Steven felt the intensity as his mother's back stiffened. "You stay away from him," she said.

Steven stopped mid-dance, "What's wrong? That's all in the past."

"Just stay away from him! There's more than you know."

Carole's reaction at seeing Nicky Bianco drew Steven back to an occasion when he lived in

Arcadia. One day after leaving the pool hall, he had mentioned Nicky's name to Carole. She had displayed the same fire, telling him, "Don't play pool with that guy." Again, she gave no reason for her demand.

Before Steven could further question his mother, Alyssa dragged her new husband away from the dance floor to cut the wedding cake. Sheila had created a three-tiered confection covered in lacy white icing fit for a king and queen. The joyous horsemen gobbled up the culinary delight – a sensory change to the liquored-up crowd. Needless to say, the horses got fed a bit later the next day. As for Steven, from what he could recall, he never remembered going home. His beautiful bride said she had to undress him on their wedding night.

The next day life did go on in the backside as the horses' needs do not take a day off. Head buzzing, Steven found himself in an intense meeting with Pops and David Moriarty.

Pops was resistant, "I don't like Rumi running the Templeton. She can run in the Grade 3 with the fillies on the same day."

But David was adamant, "Pops, she measures up with the guys. Her fractions measure up with Alex the Great. She's getting better and better with each race."

Pops was dubious, but he could not present a cogent argument to persuade even himself that the owner might be right. Rumi was getting better with each race, and her temperament was now that of a champion. She enjoyed winning. On the other hand, Pops realized his boss did not really care about

Rumi. Mr. Moriarty cared for the million dollars that came with winning the race, and as importantly, the bragging rights. And as an added gratification, he would be defeating his impertinent adversary, Jim Caldwell.

As Pops was pondering these factors, Mr. Moriarty turned to Steven.

"You're as close to Rumi as anyone, Steven. What do you think?"

Steven felt the weight of Pops's expectations in his head. "I really don't see any harm in giving her a chance. I think she can hang with the boys."

Pops chewed on a piece of hay. After some thought he spoke, "Ok, I'll train her on one condition. If for any reason I don't think Rumi is right for the race, I have the okay to scratch her.

A smiling David held out his hand, "Fine Pops."

And with that Steven prepared himself for two life altering races that would occur in six months. The Templeton Million was to be run on June 1st, and Alyssa's due date was the next day. In between buying baby equipment, Steven worked with Pops to design a grueling schedule of workouts for Rumi Rose. The star horse would run a Grade 2 event in March at Templeton against other fillies with a purse of $400,000.

"I'll see how she comes out of that race, Steven, before I'm on board with the Templeton," commented Pops.

This would be the first race since her turnaround that Alyssa would not be on Rumi's backside. Alyssa, rubbing a slight paunch in her abdomen, watched Rumi's workouts and gave pointers to her new jockey, Henry Romero.

"Henry, she loves running with other horses. When it's time to get serious with her just pull hard on her mane and enjoy the ride. Put away the whip."

Soon Henry understood the fine filly. "She's just amazing when she puts it in gear. You're right, you just enjoy the ride."

"Easy as pie Henry," said a smiling Alyssa.

And as in the past, Rumi would not let anyone but Steven hot walk her after a gallop. Even Pops was impressed. "I've never seen a horse do that in all my years," he commented.

Horse and assistant trainer walked around the shed row engaged in their special language with one another. "Girl, you know when to get serious," Steven whispered in her alert ears.

Meanwhile, the effervescent Jim Caldwell went on a media campaign to publicize the Templeton Million. "I know Rumi Rose is a good filly, but she's not in the same league as Alex the Great. In fact, I don't think she'll even finish in the money."

Not troubled by this car salesman's comments, Mr. Moriarty did not respond in kind, and simply said, "We will see on race day."

Jim Caldwell turned up the heat on his competition, "I'll bet Moriarty $100,000 that his horse doesn't even finish in the money. That's how confident I am of my horse." No one had ever referred to Rumi's distinguished owner without the "Mr."

Yet again, David Moriarty took the high road, "I'm sure Mr. Caldwell has better things to do with his money than gamble. A million-dollar win is enough for me."

Jim Caldwell then demonstrated how he had grown from owning one auto dealership to owning over forty in ten years. He did not defer to or respect anyone in his way. "My guy is the up and coming trainer at Templeton. Oh, Pops is still good, but he's seen better days."

In fact, Caldwell's trainer Mark Atkins was statistically the best trainer at Templeton. Pops was a distant second. However, part of Atkin's success was the buying spree his boss had made in recent years. Caldwell's stable now had twice the number of horses as Mr. Moriarty's. Another reason was that Pops refused to race horses at two years old.

Mark Atkins had been Pops's top assistant for several years before being lured away by Caldwell farms. If Pops was disappointed, he never showed it. He publicly congratulated the young trainer and wished him well. But some astute observers had witnessed a slight slowness in Pops's energy level since his young associate left.

Mark Atkin's first move at Calwell Farms was to make Nicky Bianco his top jockey. This team of trainer and jockey were now the top combination unit at Templeton.

The Grade 3 Princess was run on March 10 at Templeton. Rumi was one of nine entries and she got the outside post. She was the 9-5 favorite at post time, but the track was labeled as muddy due to some early morning showers. Pops cautioned his jockey, "She doesn't like the slop in her face. Try to get to the front if the pace is not too fast, and then give her free reign."

Meanwhile Steven led Rumi with a tired rope shank so he would be close to Rumi's ear. "Girl, today you're going to show them what you got." Steven was not worried about the muddy ground. He had witnessed Rumi's legs hold firm in muddy workouts. He knew Rumi enjoyed running with her equine friends, even if it meant some mud in her face.

As the gates opened on race day Henry urged Rumi into the lead. But the horse preferred to nestle next to the pack as they approached the first turn. At the half mile pole, run in a slow 50 seconds, Rumi was urged by Henry to increase the pace. Unfortunately, she was now pinned behind six horses, who were blocking her every move. Pulling on her mane, Henry instinctively felt Rumi moving wide outside the row of equine asses. "She'll never have the energy to win going this wide," thought Henry.

But he soon discovered he was wrong. As he blew past his contemporaries Henry yelled out, "See you later boys." Henry hugged tight as like a jet engine, Rumi's powerful legs propelled them faster and faster. Rumi drew away from the pack and won the Princess by six lengths.

A joyous Steven, and a plump Alyssa in maternity clothes met Rumi and Henry in the winner's circle. Rumi's head affirmed her greatness with head nods to acknowledge the cheers of the adoring crowd, and the huge smiles of the gamblers who had chosen Rumi as the winner at small odds. They loved her despite not winning lots of money.

Chapter 11: The Big Race

THE DAY AFTER RUMI'S BIG RACE a jubilant Steven found Pops in deep thought. He was staring at Rumi as if in a deep meditation. Soon, starting from her ears, Pops traced his large hands around her brilliant coat, the color of a newly minted penny. Next, he traced each appendage around her broad chest and slid to her supple legs, sleek as arrows. Rumi stood ramrod straight during this exam, her eyes gay as if saying, "You won't find anything there, Pops. Pops moved to her muscled hindquarters; his ear close to his pleading hands. Rumi obediently lifted each hoof as Pops doggedly cleaned each horseshoe that showed no ill effects of the race.

Steven had watched Pops conduct this exam, and finally asked, "You don't want her to run in the Templeton, Pops, right?"

Pops sighed, a piece of hay falling from his rounded mouth. "I don't like her running against the boys, particularly Alex the Great. She came out of this race fine. If she trains well, there's nothing more I can do."

"But what if she wins, Pops?" said an excited Steven. "She'll go down as one of the great ones."

Pops walked away in deep thought, but not before muttering almost to himself, "Is that all you want Steven?"

The next few weeks went by in a blur. The Templeton was to be run on the first Saturday in June, which was June 1st. Alyssa's due date for her baby girl was the next day, Sunday June 2nd.

"It will be a race to the wire," laughed Steven as he held Alyssa's hand on their trip to the obstetrician. As they drove home from the doctor's visit, Alyssa was simply glowing, while thinking about having a daughter. "How about we call her Stephanie, after you?" she said as she kissed Steven's cheek.

Steven, who had never really considered if he ever wanted a child deferred. "The name has done no favors for either my father or me," he told himself. To Alyssa, he responded, "How about Sophia?"

"Oh, I love it Steven. At least we have an 'S' in the name. I just know you will be a great father!"

Comments like that from Alyssa made Steven uncomfortable. No one had ever loved him unconditionally like this woman. She was generous to him in all ways – the name suggestion just a small sign of her love. She constantly bragged about Steven to their friends.

"He is going to be the best trainer in the country," she would say.

Each morning Alyssa came to the track ready for work, with her protruding belly the only sign of her pregnancy on her jockey frame. After Steven massaged Rumi's skin with a stiff wire brush,

Alyssa buffed the shiny red brown coat with a special conditioner that dappled Rumi's coat like distinctive tapestry.

One day as Steven watched another fine training gallop by Rumi – she ran five furlongs in 59 seconds – he was greeted by Rumi's owner. The oil tycoon was in as ebullient a mood as a Yankee can manage, even mentioning his opponent Jim Caldwell, whose name usually casts a shadow over his mood.

"I think we can beat Caldwell, Steve."

"I hope so boss." She has been training very well."

Mr. Moriarty's face broke into a huge smile. "I just paid $200,000 for Alex the Great's sire, Royal Alexander to impregnate Rumi Rose after this race, Steve."

Steven immediately understood the significance of this comment – this would be Rumi's last race.

"Yes, Steven, I'm going to make Rumi a broodmare. No more racing, only romance. With her pedigree I'm going to raise and run Rumi's foals and pair them with some great stallions. Royal Alexander is just the first."

"I see," said Steven, his lack of enthusiasm apparent as he saw his own training career being torpedoed.

"Don't worry Steven. I just purchased four two-year-olds for almost a million dollars. They are going to need someone to train them." Again, seeming to read Steven's mind, Mr. Moriarty continued, "I haven't told Pops about any of this. It might be best to keep this to yourself."

"Sure," said an uneasy Steven.

For the next month Rumi's training continued superbly. After her workouts Rumi would nudge Steven as they "cooled off" walking round and round the shed row yard. Rumi's muzzle would tousle Steven's hair as she reached for the sugar in his shirt pocket as if to say, "Don't worry. I got this."

Then, six weeks prior to the day of the Templeton the racing gods interrupted this unanimity. Earlier that evening Steven had marveled at Alyssa's condition. Her Irish features glowed as brightly as Rumi's coat, the only hint of her pregnancy a twenty-pound breadbasket around her belly. Even Alyssa's taut legs looked like they could exercise Rumi, Steven foolishly thought as he gazed at his wife.

At 3 a.m. Steven was suddenly prodded awake and beheld a face that hardly resembled the one he had admired just hours earlier. Sweat poured from his wife's face, matting her red hair onto her red bloated features.

"I don't know what's happening Stevie," she cried, and with that she became semi-conscious.

Fifteen minutes later Steven was carrying his delirious wife, still in her pajamas, into the emergency room of the nearest hospital. She was immediately taken from Steven and rushed into acute care. A dazed Steven was left alone surrounded by forlorn emergency room patients.

Three hours had gone by before a doctor emerged and in a serious tone asked Steven to sit down. "Your wife has pre-eclampsia. It is a pregnancy related condition that causes extremely high blood pressure in some women. Your wife's blood pressure is now 140/90, which is extremely high. We have her on intravenous medication to lower it. We are concerned about damage to the kidneys, or a possible stroke if we cannot get this hypertension under control.

A look of concern over Steven's face, he asked, "But what about the baby?"

"Right now the baby seems fine. But obviously anything affecting Alyssa can affect the baby. The next twenty-four hours are crucial, Mr. Ricci."

"Can I see my wife?" asked Steven. Steven was then led into a small room where a sleeping Alyssa was quietly lying on a hospital bed. Bags filled with fluid hung around her as an array of machines and tubes produced sounds and numbers that had no meaning for an anxious Steven.

Steven sat with his wife for the next 24 hours. He tried to read the face of every doctor and nurse who came in to review the information being spit out by these strange sounding machines. All anyone would say to Steven was, "She's stable."

After what seemed like hours to the sleeping Steven, he was awakened from his chair by the sound of a familiar voice. Alyssa' obstetrician Dr. Savage was standing over him smiling. "I think the worst is over Steven. Alyssa's blood pressure is still high, but stable, and not a danger to her organs at present. As importantly, the baby has not been in distress. However, this is a vibrant situation, and we still have to monitor her closely."

"Thank you doctor. How long will she have to be here?" said a subdued Steven.

"Your wife's body has been through a lot. We want her to stay here for the next three weeks where we can monitor her closely. We can take the baby by Caesarian at that time, give or take a few days."

So for the next weeks Steven's regiment was, sleeping on a cot in Alyssa's room each night, awakening at dawn to attend to Rumi's needs such as grooming and feeding, and then returning to the hospital late morning before Rumi's workouts.

Naturally, a tired Alyssa worried only about Steven. "Honey, you are going to burn yourself out," she would tell him. "Look at everyone here taking care of me. Go home and get some real rest."

An obstinate Steven would have none of that. "I'll be with Rumi in the morning, but Pops, Owie and the crew can pick up the slack and work her out."

But one part of the racing equation was not alright. Sensing her boss's absence, Rumi proceeded to give only half-hearted efforts on the exercise track. Normally prancing on her toes around the shed row, thriving on the affection of others, Rumi was lethargic. She moved with her head down and oblivious to her surroundings. Pops decided not to tell Steven of Rumi's training demeanor.

Three weeks before the day of the Templeton, Dr. Savage had a meeting with the Ricci's. "Today is going to be your daughter's birthday. All her vitals appear good and her lungs look fully developed."

A nervous Alyssa, hand in hand with Steven asked Dr. Savage, "You don't think Sophia being born three weeks early will hurt her?"

"No," said the doctor. "She's almost seven pounds. We will watch her here for a few days, and Alyssa you can stay here with her. You're still weak, and while your blood pressure is stable, it could rise again."

And with that the fatherless Steven experienced the joy of watching his child come into this world. An anxious Alyssa asked, "Steven, who does she look like?" as a professional whisked the baby away to clean her up. Immediately other professionals worked to get Alyssa sewn up. Alyssa came out of surgery surprisingly well – her blood pressure returning to normal soon after giving birth.

Finally little Sophia was placed into her mother's welcoming arms. Both parents were filled with emotion as they viewed their precious baby. Then with tears in his eyes Steven whispered, "She's so beautiful Alyssa."

The next day Steven appeared at the track with handfuls of cigars for the backside workers. Rumi playfully rebuffed hers, but responded as if she was aware that Steven was a dad. Her head high, ears alert, she folded her chin to her chest as she pranced in her stall. Steven immediately observed that Rumi's taut stomach muscles which normally tapered into her hindquarters no longer existed.

"She's carrying an extra five pounds around her midsection Steven. She simply walked through her workouts without you around," said Pops.

"Do you think we should still run her Pops?" asked a concerned Steven.

Pops surprised Steven with his response. "Since this is her last race, I think with you back we can get rid of that pouch in two weeks."

Steven should not have been surprised since few secrets remain in the backside gossip. "I know I should have told you Pops, but it's been crazy."

Pops interrupted him, "You did nothing wrong Steven. I also know about the boss buying all those two-year-olds he wants to race."

Steven could not look Pops in the eye. "I didn't tell Moriarty I would train them."

Pops took a deep breath. "I know but you will. Let's just get through this race."

So, with Alyssa's blessing, Steven devoted himself to a weight loss training regiment for Rumi. Seemingly eager to race with Steven by her side, Rumi had three hard workouts in the next seven days. She pranced with Steven in her hotwalks without her customary sugar, as Steven told her, "No girl, just oats, barley and hay this week."

Three days before the Templeton Million Pops, David Moriarty and Steven huddled in Rumi's stall. Absent any other emergency, this was their last chance to decide on Rumi's withdrawal from the race. Recalling his agreement with his trainer, Mr. Moriarty addressed Pops, "What do you say, Pops?"

Rubbing his horse-beaten hands over Rumi's stomach, Pops deliberated, "She looks fit, but I don't like all that weight loss in the last week."

Pops then turned to Steven, "What do you think kid?"

"I think she's fine."

And with that Pops walked away, and the race was on.

If this group had known the intentions of a jockey not present in this discussion, their decision might have been different. For Nicky Bianco, the jockey for Alex the Great held a grudge. And not just one. Nicky hadn't forgotten or forgiven the fact that Steven Ricci had ratted him out to the police years ago, or that he had stollen his girl Alyssa. Also, Nicky was tired of all the attention this filly Rumi Rose was getting, when he knew his stallion was head and shoulders the better horse. Nicky also had a personal secret that motivated him.

So later that day, when the post positions were announced, Nicky saw a way to ensure both victory and revenge. Alex the Great was given post #10 in the eleven-horse field. Rumi Rose had the #11 post, the extreme outside post. This was perfect for what Nicky had in mind.

The weather for the day of the Templeton Million could not have been better. An electric crowd of 60,000 enjoyed the sun-baked track – a beer in one hand and a rolled program in the other. The Templeton was the last race of the day, the tenth and final race. Steven watched as Rumi's alert ears listened to the groans and cheers of the bettors in race after race. In Steven's eyes, Rumi was relaxed and eager to perform.

Following the ninth race, Pops and Steven watched as Owie secured the girth snugly around Rumi's belly and adjusted jockey Henry Romero's saddle. For the third time, Pops repeated his instructions to Henry.

"You know she likes to run in the pack, but watch it if the fractions are too fast. Keep your feet on her dashboard. Let her set her own pace. At quarter pole let the reins out and give her a tug. She'll know what to do."

Twenty minutes before the race the eleven horses walk calmly – oblivious to the blares of the trumpet, and the clamors of the photographers, and eager bettors. Alex the Great, eleven hundred pounds of chestnut flesh in perfect proportion, prances like an equine King. Even Steven has to admire the steed's apparent declaration, "I'm first, who is running for second place?" This grand horse's jockey Nicky Bianco displays a warrior glare at Steven.

"The Templeton Million is off and running!" the announcer roars to the robust fans. But Steven does not hear it, because his eyes are on Rumi. Within the second step out of the gate Rumi is almost forced to her knees, Henry artfully hanging on for dear life. Alex, with a hard kick from Nicky Bianco on his left flank drives hard into Rumi's midsection. Like a drunken marathoner Rumi collects her four legs by running sideways to her right. Her bettors groan as she is all alone in the middle of the track.

Ahead of her are ten horses led by Alex the Great. A trio of horses run a length behind Alex as they enter the backstretch in a rather slow opening quarter mile of twenty-five seconds. Steadying herself, Rumi sets her sights on her competition, picking off one horse after another. At the half mile Rumi is in fifth place. As the pace quickens Nicky decides to make history with Alex the Great – not just win the race, but win it in record time. As Alex fluidly skims the rail, completing the third quarter mile in twenty-two seconds, the second and third horse gamely dig in and pull nearly alongside Alex. But Nicky remains cool and urges another gear on his steed. His hard charging competitors' heads begin to bobble and then dip despite their jockeys' urgent rousing.

Nicky is seemingly alone for the last quarter mile, oblivious to the roars for a hard charging filly. Coming from six wide Rumi has effortlessly passed all her competitors and with a furlong to go has set her sights on Alex. Hurling forward with ease, Henry's back flat and straight, he pulls on Rumi's unruly black mane.

Nicky does not have to look over his right shoulder. He can feel the relentless galloping to his right. Rumi on the bit, her sleek head straight and focused, pulls nose to nose with Alex. Like two equine locomotives one horse, then the other pulls ahead as the finish line looms. Screaming horse players are caught in this passionate play of driving horseflesh doing what they love.

Here's what the frenzied bettors heard from the track announcer. "Oh my what a race. At the quarter pole these two incredible athletes will not give an inch. Rumi pokes her head, but no, here comes Alex again. They're going neck and neck to the wire. It's too close to call. Wait! No, I can't believe it…she's down. She's down!"

As the finish line approaches, Nicky glances at his human competition, Henry. Rumi's focused jockey gives a final urge as they arrive at the finish line together. Henry knows he has won, even if it is by a nose. But before he can raise his whip in elation, he starts sliding to the ground, still on Rumi's back.

"It was as if I was on a sandcastle being swept into the sea by a giant wave." he recalled later. Confused, Henry eventually rests eye to eye with the lifeless body of Rumi Rose.

Chapter 12: Rumi Runs Her Heart Out

STEVEN FOR YEARS LATER would replay this race in his head. ………

The air was crackling with anticipation as two equine pistons alternated muzzles to the finish line. Alyssa tugged deliriously on Steven's arms. The reserved David Moriarty jumped up and down like a school boy. Sophia, screamed, her voice swallowed up by the thousands of screeching voices in the crowd. Steven saw Alex the Great's head bobble spitting his tongue to the side. The horse spit out his bit as if saying, "I can't believe this girl is going to beat me."

Steven's joy soon turned to grief, overwhelming his senses to the point that it distorted his reality. Crossing the finish line, Rumi slid like a copper baserunner, sliding not into home plate, but gliding just beyond the finish line, and then descending downward. At first, Steven didn't see that – he saw Rumi prancing joyously. He had to rub his eyes to see the lifeless form quickly being passed by a dispirited Alex the Great. Almost catatonic, he didn't hear Alyssa pleading, "Stevie, go down there!"

A few minutes later Steven had Rumi's beautiful head in his lap, Rumi's lifeless eyes staring straight at Steven. The track veterinarian shook her head, her eyes moist, like all those viewing this scene. Yards past the finish line, both trainer and horse sat in racing loam, surrounded by ponies, staff, and thousands of stunned patrons. A photographer took pictures of the scene, which was later distributed nationwide, spurring this debate: "Is horseracing fair to the animal?"

Healthy jockey Henry Romero cried on Steven's shoulder. "It was as if Rumi did not want me to get hurt," he said. The veteran of numerous horse falls, Henry later recalled that he had never experienced such a slide. He had heard cannon and sesamoid bones crack underneath him, but this was different. "It was as if Rumi knew she'd won, and her job was done."

A raspy voiced David Moriarty, tie askew, accepted the Templeton Million trophy alone in the Winner's Circle. The once cheering crowd, now silent as they watched the ceremony. A bed of roses, which should have been around Rumi's neck, sat forlornly in the Winner's Circle. A tongue-tied Mr. Moriarty could only offer, "Rumi should be feeding on them now."

Steven went to the backside to find Pops. A foreboding Pops, declining to sit in the owner's box, preferred to listen to the race announcer's call on the backside. Steven found him as the older man was removing his eyeglasses, since tears had blurred his vision. "I'm sorry Pops," stammered Steven.

Silence permeated the air between the old trainer and his protégé. Finally, the man who had seen everything in his horse racing days spoke solemnly, "Horses are born to run Steven. Rumi was doing what God blessed her to do. But it's up to us to harness the horse's love. If this wasn't her last race I would have stopped it. She wasn't in the best shape, but she gave her heart to you."

With that, Pops got up to leave, but turned to say one more thing, "You're in charge now Steven. I'm going away for a while. I hope you remember this lesson."

Over the next few days Steven learned that Pops was right about Rumi's heart. A necropsy confirmed that the vet could not find any reason for her collapse. Steven knew the truth: Rumi had run her heart out for him.

But Steven could not dwell on this for long. Arrangements were made to have Rumi buried in Templeton's infield, the first horse to be so honored. As he reviewed Rumi's last race again and again, Steven's anger at Nicky Bianco surfaced. In fact, Alyssa would call him to bed, but he rebuffed her. "In a moment," he would say as he replayed over and over a grainy image in which it appeared Nicky deliberately kicked Alex on his left flank. Steven convinced himself, "Rumi would not have died if she didn't have to run an extra furlong."

Alex's owner, Jim Caldwell, conveniently sent Nicky to a California racetrack to work with other horses he owned. In a fury, Steven filed an objection to Templeton's stewards about the negligent ride. David Moriarty later told Steven, "Caldwell used his influence to squash the complaint Steven."

Mr. Moriarty, the old blue blood owner, did not grieve Rumi for long. "I got a crop of yearlings coming up Steven. You're in charge now. I want them up and running as two year olds."

Since Pops never raced two year olds, Steven needed help with these babies. He turned to his trusted foreman Owie, who now worked for him.

"I compare two year olds to ten year old kids Steven. They are starting to feel their oats, but are not fully aware of all the consequences. Just be patient with them and you'll be fine. We got a year to figure 'em out."

So as the four horses that cost Mr. Moriarty collectively over a million dollars came off the van, Steven carefully examined the young stock. As he slowly ran his fingers over a white-gray colt's leg, the horse's ghost like elegant head lifted up and stared at Steven. At first Steven thought the horse was going to nip him. His eyes, however, conveyed, "Hey, be careful down there." While all of the horses had regal lineage, and possessed stunning beauty, something about this one told Steven that this horse was special. An ironic notion, because the horse was short, legs slightly bowed, but with a massive chest. *Hmm, he just might grow into that body,* thought Steven.

Mr. Moriarty came to view his equine purchases, "Well, what do you think Steven?"

"They all look great, Mr. Moriarty."

"Good, I want them making money for me next year. I wasn't going to buy the gray. I don't like the white-gray coat. It reminds me of ghosts. He's kind of runty. But at the time, Pops insisted I buy him."

Later in the day Steven studied the breeding of the white-gray colt named Majestic Max. His father, Magnificent Max was a European winner of several grass Grade 1 handicaps. His mother, Alexis was a multiple stakes winner on the dirt. She largely won on short distances of 5 to 6 furlongs, as she was extremely fast out of the gate. Steven thought to himself, "Max might have a problem with distances over a mile, if he takes after his mom. Or he might have a preference for grass. I'll have to figure that out.

So with the addition of these four horses, Steven had a stable of another 25 horses that Mr. Moriarty wanted on the track. Without Pops to help, Steven's days as head trainer began at 4 a.m. and often ended after dark.

As Alyssa was still recovering and Sophia was only two months old, Steven suggested Alyssa's parents come live with them. So Bill Conley, a trainer who competed against Pops years before, and his wife Ginny moved in. This freed Steven from any guilt he felt about being away so much.

But truthfully, Steven did not feel that much guilt once his in-laws moved in. He was just too busy to think about it. In addition to training Mr. Moriarty's stable, Steven had to travel to look at new acquisitions. Also, the aggressive owner wanted Steven to race his horses in premier races from New York to California. The young trainer was becoming a national presence on the racing scene, frequently interviewed before and after races such as the Kentucky Derby and the Belmont Stakes.

In that chaotic first year of training, Steven was away from home more than he was there. At first Alyssa was supportive of her husband. Healthy again, she requested at least one "date night" each week. But even that didn't always happen.

"The baby doesn't even recognize you Stevie," she complained. "I know you're working hard, but we need you."

"I'll try honey, but look, it will get better."

A horseman, Bill Conley told his daughter, "Don't push him honey."

Alyssa listened to her father, and tried not to henpeck her husband, even when he missed "date nights" week after week. When Steven was home, his head seemed to be somewhere else. When he picked up Sophia, she often cried and reacted as if a stranger was holding her. And more concerning, Steven did not seem to care about this. "Here, you take her," he would impatiently say to Alyssa or her parents when the baby inevitably screamed.

Never once in that first year did Steven get on the floor and play with this beautiful child. "This emerging character that we created," Alyssa told herself later.

One other thing bothered Alyssa. Steven was not concerned with intimacy of any kind. When they did have sex, she felt that he was just trying to oblige her sexually. A virgin when Sophia was conceived and inexperienced in lovemaking, Alyssa blamed herself. Many nights she lay in bed until 1 a.m. in a black lace nightgown waiting for Steven to return from some racing event.

"I'm too tired honey," Steven would say after showering and crawling into bed with is back to her.

By the second year of this behavior, Alyssa did become the henpecking wife she once feared. Her parents, now back in their own home, were not there to smooth things over, and the young couple's arguments became louder and more intense. Steven's constant defenses, "You don't get it, it will get better," became "Maybe you should have married someone else."

And what bothered Alyssa even more was that Steven didn't seem to care that two year old Sophia barely recognized her father. In fact, before Bill Conley left, Sophia had called him "Daddy."

Alyssa snapped at Steve, "You care more for those damn horses than you do for your own flesh and blood."

And one night after another explosive argument, Steven uttered words he didn't apologize for, "Those horses give me more enjoyment than you."

To Alyssa, that comment summed up her marriage. Steven had changed, or maybe he was like that, and she had been blinded by love. Regardless, that comment essentially ended the marriage. They remained together for another year, like two strangers passing unaware of each other.

When Sophia turned three, Alyssa decided to get back on the track as an exercise rider. Each morning after the babysitter arrived, Alyssa would arrive in the dark to gallop horses owned by Jim Caldwell. This brought her into more contact with

Nicky Bianco, now Templeton's top jockey, after his short sabbatical following Rumi Rose's death. In fact, since Nicky's return, Steven and Nicky walked past each other without so much as a glance. For Steven this was strategic. Concerned about his growing national reputation, he would not lower himself to confront such an adversary. But privately Steven vowed to get his revenge for Rumi Rose's death. However, unbeknownst to Steven, a far greater revenge was already in motion by his old friend Nicky Bianco.

In between morning gallops, Nicky would buy coffee for Alyssa at the canteen. A protective Sheila had sized things up immediately and refused to acknowledge Nicky. As the top jockey at Templeton, he was not needed to exercise horses at daybreak. In fact, most jockeys thought the job was beneath them. But Nicky had a different agenda – to win a heart.

It seemed the frustrated young mom now had a consort to share all of her emotional needs. And Nicky was not just anyone. He was her first boyfriend, who knew her dreams as a young girl – dreams that had turned into a marital nightmare. She was now essentially a single mom, worrying about her future.

Slowly, Nicky maneuvered himself to be more than an emotional sounding board. He would ask questions. "How could a father abandon such a beautiful little girl like Sophia?"

It was as if Nicky was drawing in Alyssa to her own self-evident conclusions. Soon Alyssa realized, with Nicky's help, she needed a divorce so she could get on with her life.

And one day after driving Alyssa to a doctor's appointment, Nicky put himself into that future. During the ride after the appointment Nicky boldly stated, "Alyssa, you almost died giving birth, and Steven abandoned you. I've never stopped loving you. I will always be there for you."

"Didn't you feel the same way about Tiffany?"

"Are you kidding? She dumped me months ago for some hot shot from Harvard. She was nothing to me Alyssa. No, you and I are soulmates. I realized that you are all I ever wanted."

"But you never acted like you even cared that I dated Steven," said a stunned Alyssa.

Reeling in his prey like an experienced fisherman, Nicky offered, "I always knew Steven was a loser, and eventually you would see it."

Now Nicky offered the coup-d'etat: "You know Steven's having an affair with David's wife Gloria, right?"

"Whaaat!" shrieked Alyssa.

"Sure, the whole backside knows about the affair. We just figured you knew."

Chapter 13: The Divorce

THE TRUTH WAS THE WHOLE BACKSIDE did not know about Steven's affair with Gloria Moriarty. The couple, especially Steven, had hoped to keep it a secret. He knew his future as a trainer was kaput once his boss knew he was screwing his wife. But Gloria had told him, "Don't worry, my husband is only interested in making money and admiring horses." She assured Steven that he was not the first of her lovers, but added, "Steven, you are the best. Anyway, my husband won't fire you even if he finds out."

Steven did not pursue the relationship with Gloria. No, he was actually having lots of action with many women. A burgeoning player in the hierarchy of the horse world, Steven found women increasingly available to him. Cocktail parties post-race with dipsomaniac rich horse owners found few of their wives home alone.

For Steven sex was a great way to briefly relieve the pressure of entering this rarified world of horse racing. Mr. Moriarty, once free from the conservative reigns of Pops, pushed Steven to enter his horses in stakes races throughout the country. Steven had to gain eligibility to these races, and condition, exercise, feed and otherwise soothe these pampered equine athletes. Bored females often provided him temporary solace from these pressures.

Initially, Steven felt a tinge of guilt abandoning Alyssa after all that they had gone through together. But three years after Sophia's birth, that guilt was a very distant emotion. It was replaced by justification that the demands of his job would lead to greater financial rewards for his family. He was now earning a salary of over $200,000 a year, with bonuses whenever one of his horses won. In many ways Steven felt like a different person from the one who had married Alyssa. He was now present in a world he had always dreamed about, and felt he deserved.

It was Gloria who initiated the affair with Steven. At first she would show up in a stable to view her namesake Gal Gloria. Seven year old Gloria, now as calm as a baby, often crawled to the finish line like one. When the horse was retired after a nice career, the boss's wife Gloria still appeared at the stable. Even at middle age she always garnered the attention of the workers as she made her entrance into the stables. Perfectly coiffed hair complimented tight chic dresses matched by high heels that had to be maneuvered around horse manure.

One day, wearing perfume so strong that even the horses' noses twitched, she asked Steven for a ride home. With a multitude of tasks to accomplish Steven asked Owie to take her home. But Gloria had other plans.

"You're not going to refuse your boss's wife are you, Steven?" she asked as her red dragon fingernails brushed her hair aside from her flawless features.

On the ride home Gloria suggested that they get some lunch. Steven now knew not to defer. Gloria was immediately greeted by the restaurant staff, and they were seated in a cozy booth.

"We will have two old-fashions," she ordered for them both.

"Of course," smiled her favorite waiter.

"You know Steven, my husband is very proud of you, especially considering where you came from. Everyone seems to like you."

"Thanks, Mrs. Moriarty. Your husband has been very good to me."

"Actually he was always looking for someone to replace Pops. My husband thought his time has passed."

The rest of the meal went on like this, superficial discussion about horseracing in general. Still nursing his first drink, Steven sat back as glassy-eyed Gloria ordered her third old fashion. Leaning into him she asked, "So what does Steve want out of this horse racing business?"

Discarding the careful veneer he adopted with most people, Steven replied honestly, "I want to be like your husband. I want to own horses one day, and not have to worry about money for the rest of my life. That's what I want."

Gloria almost spit out her third old fashion with that comment. "No Steven. You don't want to be like that man at all. He doesn't care about me, or anyone else. We haven't slept in the same room for years. He's not interested in sex. And he doesn't care if I sleep with anyone else."

So began the affair with insatiable Gloria. She had a higher libido than Steven, which he thought was incredible. Often, she would show up in the evenings when Steven would be working in the stable. Kicking off her expensive high heels, she would insist on a "romp in the hay."

Continued insistence from the spoiled wife eventually turned Steven off; her demands combined with his time consumed with her abandoned husband. The two men were continually on the road, buying yearlings or traveling with their horses to racetracks all over the country. On one such trip, when Steven was in the passenger seat of Mr. Moriarty's Mercedes, David, looking straight ahead, addressed the issue.

"I know you're having an affair with my wife. You're not the first. Watch out. She can be very demanding."

Steven, eyes forward, did not know what to say, so he said nothing. But he told himself, that was enough of this crazy situation. There was plenty of other women to satisfy his needs.

Steven's divorce was a relatively easy affair. He did not deny the relationship with Gloria Moriarty when confronted. Anger replaced sadness for Alyssa, who threw Steven's clothes to the curb. Humiliated that her peers on the backside knew of the betrayal, the normally kindhearted woman conjured up no defense for her husband's actions. They had shared poor Rumi's experience together, and, to Alyssa that made them soulmates. But now she understood that Steven did not have a soul.

Alyssa, being a good mother, was wise enough not to involve Sophia in this disappointment of her father. In fact, this was the only hiccup in the divorce. Steven agreed to give Alyssa the couple's home, generous child support, and rehabilitative alimony. Sophia was now three and a half years old, and Alyssa wanted Steven to have overnight visitation weekly with his daughter. However, he wanted only Sunday afternoon visitation. The couple eventually agreed to two overnight visitations a month, but in the first year of the divorce these visits did not occur. In fact, he normally visited with his daughter only one Sunday per month.

Steven justified these cancellations as necessary for him to pay his child support. He was working 60 to 70 hours per week. It's not that he didn't love Sophia, but he had spent so little time with her that he didn't know what to do with the toddler. One time he left her with Owie for the day after Sophia got lost in an unlocked horse's stall.

Again, Alyssa was very tolerant of the situation. She would tell a crying Sophia, after another cancellation, "Your dad loves you, but he just has to work a lot."

What she could not tolerate was Steven's last minute cancellations, fifteen minutes before he was to pick Sophia up. Sophia would look out the window waiting for her dad, and then would burst into tears when her mother told her he wasn't coming.

"I swear Steven if you do that again, I will go to court to suspend any contact," Alyssa screamed at him over the phone. A contrite Steven then promised to give fair notice before he cancelled.

In truth, Alyssa was battling another wager at home. When she lambasted Steven, Nicky was right there with his comments, "That bastard doesn't even deserve visitation!"

That was her only complaint about dating Nicky Bianco again. He was attentive, finding any available time when he was not racing to be with Alyssa. He was wonderful with Sophia. He bought her a tiny racing helmet and goggles and rode her carefully around the track on his mounts.

A smiling Alyssa would tell herself, "At least Sophia has one good male in her life." At least she thought so.

Chapter 14: Sophia's Struggles

A YEAR AFTER ALYSSA'S DIVORCE, any doubts about another bad choice for a husband disappeared. In addition to being a top jockey at Templeton, Nicky Bianco was a top potential husband. When he popped the question to Alyssa, she had only one query before acquiescing. Even though she doubted Steven's accusations that Nicky had deliberately sabotaged Rumi's ride, she had to know the truth.

"Did you force Alex the Great into Rumi Rose at the gate?"

Nicky's eyes moistened as he replied with all earnestness, "I swear Alyssa. I would never do anything like that. I cried when Rumi died."

Swept up by his sincerity, and her objective analysis that "second time shame on me" Alyssa said yes to the kneeling Nicky as he held out a three carrot diamond engagement ring. The couple were married a month later at Jim Caldwell's private golf club. Alyssa insisted on a small affair, unlike her first wedding. Five year old Sophia was the ring bearer. Some attendees lamented that Sophia had the Italian features of her dad, rather than the red curls of the Irish lassie, the radiant bride Alyssa.

Steven had a hard time controlling his emotions, knowing that a hated former friend would be sharing a home with Sophia. He saw the malicious side of Nicky, and Steven knew he would go to his grave believing that Nicky had killed Rumi Rose. It took the reserved David Moriarty to replace logic with emotion.

"Let it go Steven. She will always be your daughter, not his."

Steven told himself his renewed interest in Sophia was age related. For whatever reason, around the time Sophia turned five, Steven exercised his visits more regularly. Nicky told Alyssa, "He sees her now because he knows I'm a better father than him."

Sophia seemed to enjoy being around horses as much as her father, and that delighted Steven. She roamed around the stables high fiving all the groomers. She especially loved the exotic looking Majestic Max. Both father and daughter shared admiration for what the bettors called the "White Ghost."

When Mr. Moriarty had purchased this horse as a yearling Steven believed it was a poor choice. A gray male with a small frame, he had a large chest, but knees that were ungainly. The condition, called "bench knees" is when the knees are closer together than the chest, leading to later leg problems. He also had a slight conformational fault known as "swayback." Normally, from the horse's shoulder to the hip where the saddle sits is a straight line, called a "top line." In Max's case there was a slight dip in the back, making for an unsightly appearance. The horse had been overlooked by many, but in one of his last acts Pops told Mr. Moriarty, "Buy him. He's got a good eye."

Pops knew his horses, because at two years Max had become amazingly symmetrical, and as well-proportioned as Arnold Schwarzenegger in his prime. Unusually large now, fourteen hands high, Max had a robust frame with six-pack cuts from his chest to hindquarters that sat atop sculpted legs. A well arched neck supported handsome porcelain features to portray a regal effect.

But it was Max's coat that left mouths agape. While gray horses are similar to left-handed humans at 10% of the population, very few thoroughbreds are white. Max's coat at age three was pure ivory. Max was a standout on the racetrack, his white mane flowing in every direction in contrast to the colors around him – the brown loam of the track surface, the green evergreens in the center of the racetrack, and his black and chestnut competitors.

Steven Ricci came to understand that this was a mercurial animal. Dwarfing other stallions, Max acted like their bossy big brother on the track. Steven remembered Pops's words that in the wild these horses have various personalities – submissive, obstinate or controlling. Majestic Max would have been their dominant stallion. Max's domination extended to people. The horse ate when he wanted, exercised when he wanted, and even ran on the racetrack only when it suited him.

As a two year old Max won his first two races handily. And as importantly, he showed he could run at any pace that evolved. In his maiden race he led from start to finish, winning by six lengths. In his second race, Max was trapped on the rail. Without prompting from his jockey Henry, Max squirted through the smallest of horse openings as if saying to his foes, "See you later!"

An excited David Moriarty then entered Max in a Grade 1 race in New York. Upset that his regiment at Templeton was disturbed Max refused to gallop when he got to the new track. Henry resigned himself, "This horse does what he wants. I can't get him to exercise if he doesn't want to."

Steven saw the quirky signs of this magnificent animal. Max ate twice as much as his other horses, and combined with his reluctance to exercise, was prone to put on weight. He even catnapped during the day after refusing to exercise. Surprisingly, a pudgy Max still almost won the New York race on talent alone, but out of gas, finished a distant second. In his next race a stubborn Max refused to put his powerful hindquarters in gear, like a two year old refusing spinach. Max finished dead last.

And this start/stop racing career plagued Steven for the next several months. Steven tried every strategy Pops had given him to motivate the animal. As a narcissist himself, Steven came to realize that Max could only be motivated by Max. If Max refused to gallop on an exercise workout, Steven instructed the jockeys of his other hard working colts to taunt him. Sweat pouring from their nostrils, they would go nose to nose with Max.

This and other strategies Steven developed led to Max finally "getting it" at age five. For the first time Max put forth consistent efforts in four consecutive races. He won a Grade 2 and Grade 1 in California on a west coast swing with ease. Steven would whisper in Max's ear before and after the race.

"You're the best Max. Even the other horses know it."

And Steven was not lying. Even in the paddock, prior to the race, the other equine competitors saw a bruising animal whose legs could eat up more dirt than theirs. Like a prizefighter realizing his opponent was beaten at the touch of the gloves, Max often won in the paddock.

Steven was not the only one thrilled with Max's success. David Moriarty who had not won the Templeton Million since Rumi Rose, was obsessed.

"This is the year Steven," he would assert.

Sophia was also galvanized by this large white animal. On Steven's shoulder's she constantly tickled Max's unruly snow white mane. Courtesy of Steven, Sophia slept with a stuffed toy horse she called Max, naturally snow white.

"Nicky tells me Max will lose, but I don't believe him dad."

On that note Steven could not have been happier in his relationship with his daughter, whom he now saw regularly. Steven lived a spartan existence, devoted to training for Mr. Moriarty's large stable. Despite the tension about Nicky's presence in his daughter's home, he had an excellent working relationship with Alyssa. He saw Sophia two weekends per month overnight, as well as several times during the week. His best days were awakening with Sophia sitting on his bed asking if she could join him with her stuffed Max.

At the stables, Steven's staff welcomed the boss's daughter with the dark brown curls and her snowy stuffed animal like one of their own. They grew to call the child, "the little queen".

The Templeton Million's approach in six months happened to coincide with another life-changing event. Little Sophia was going to have a little brother. Yes, Alyssa informed Steven that she was going to have a baby, a son. Some three months pregnant she also informed Steven that hard as it was he would have to communicate more with Nicky about visitation.

"Because I had endometriosis with Sophia, I'll have to have a lot of bedrest with this baby, particularly in the last trimester, Stevie."

So with two major events occurring, Steven would have to manage his time more carefully. He regularly saw Sophia on alternate weekends, but less and less during the week. Sophia would beg, "Daddy, why can't I see you more?" But Max had a huge prep race in California three months prior to the Templeton. Tempestuous as Max was about travel, Steven had to get him adjusted to California a month before the race.

He even had to miss one of his overnight visits with Sophia during that period. Nicky was ready to criticize him in front of Sophia with, "Don't let it happen again!" Steven ignored Nicky's remarks, but often he had trouble even speaking to Sophia by phone. Nicky would tell him she was sleeping. Again, Steven ignored these comments because he learned Alyssa's pregnancy was going smoothly. He would get his revenge on Nicky another time.

Following Max's big win in California, where he dominated the competition, Max was installed as the favorite for the upcoming Templeton Million. After a brief rest Max resumed his workout schedule in top form. David Moriarty could not be happier. His nemesis Jim Caldwell had a top stallion in the race also. Mister Parker had defeated Max a year earlier. Steven wasn't worried about Mister Parker or his jockey Nicky Bianco. Max had been in one of his stubborn moods during that period. Now he was exercising hard, almost daring horses to run with him in the early mornings. Max was so focused that he didn't pull a tantrum limited to denying his second feedings. Steven was convinced that no horse could defeat this superb animal but Max himself.

With the Templeton Million a month away, Steven received an unexpected call from Alyssa. Sounding strangely remote Alyssa told Steven he should not see Sophia until the big race was over. As much as he wanted to see his daughter, he silently agreed it was the right idea. Between media interviews, prerace parties, and training he was stretched to the limit.

"I can call Sophia, though, right Alyssa?"

Alyssa hesitated and Steven later swore he heard a voice coaching her in the background. "Ah…probably not a good idea, Stevie. She'll just want to see you more."

Steven reluctantly agreed, primarily not to upset his pregnant ex-wife. “Okay, but I want to get extra time after the race.”

“Sure, Stevie.”

With a week to go and everything as calm as Max’s cumulous cloud exterior, Steven saw a storm brewing. Almost imperceptible to anyone else, Steven observed that Max’s gait was off. The stallion was reluctant to put full weight on his right foreleg. It was slightly inflamed and mildly hot to the touch. His vet said he had a slight case of laminitis, inflammation in the laminae. The laminae are structures that connect the hoof walls to the bone. Infections are common. “The good news,” said the vet, “is that the infection is mild. The bad news is that even mild infections in that area could cause a bit of pain in Max.

Steven’s first reaction was to cancel Max’s appearance in the Templeton Million. David Moriarty was apoplectic – the blueblood whacking his fedora on his knee. “Just my luck!”

“Boss, Max has a lot of great rides in him,” said a cautious Steven.

“Yeah, sure, but he might not have many more chances to beat Mister Parker.

Steven could not argue with the veterinarian’s assessment. But his boss said, “Rest him today Steven, then give him a workout. We will see how hot his leg is after that.”

The next morning Max did have a good workout, and seemed to move well. On the day prior to the race Steven felt Max’s leg. There was no inflammation and temperature in the joint. Reluctantly, Steven agreed to race Max.

The day of the Templeton Million turned out dark and gray. By the sixth race the thousands of bettors were using racing forms to shield themselves from the heavy rain, unless they cozied up to the smart bettors who brought umbrellas.

At the end of the ninth race the muck on the race course had slithered into the infield. The jockeys, their colorful silks caked in mud, urged waterlogged horses to the finish line. Post numbers smothered in grime left bettors scrambling to determine who won each race.

As post time for the featured race approached, David Moriarty and Steven experienced different emotions. David was excited and fixated on the $10,000 wager he had placed on Max. Steven was guarded and focused on Max's head which dipped lower than usual as if to say, "I can't believe I have to run in this shit." Steven knew that Max hated to run in the rain. He had only one victory in three attempts on a muddy track. But Steve also knew that Max realized this was a special race.

In the paddock Steven reviewed the racing strategy with jockey Henry Romero. "Try to get him to the lead," said Steven knowing the difficulty of the strategy. Max had been assigned the outside post – post ten. He would have to cross over nine other hard charging animals to make the lead. Henry knew that using too much energy too soon would not have much horse left for the finish a mile and a quarter later.

Steven, knowing Henry's thoughts said, "Just don't let him get much mud in his face. He hates that."

The gates opened as the crowds cheered for their favorites. At first Max hesitated a bit, as if getting his feet used to the river of mud. Three hard charging stallions attacked the rail led by Mister Parker. Boxed by the leaders Max trailed the pace in seventh place. Henry felt Max's head pop every time a hoof deposited another mud stool in his face. For Henry, after removing mud streaked goggles, considered only one option, "Let's go outside!" Then yelling at the jockeys pinning him to the rail he screamed, "Get outta my way!"

By the 3/8's pole Max had picked up one horse after another, so far outside that these jockeys were surprised to be passed by a mud enhanced, brown white machine. Only one horse remained, the game Mister Parker. First four lengths behind, then three, then two, Henry felt the familiar surge of drive that jockeys love. All set to enjoy the passing of Nicky Bianco, Henry sensed victory, and hung low to the turbo-charged Max's neck.

And then, two hundred yards from the finish line, the engine turned into a two-cylinder Volkswagen. Henry experienced a horse struggling to maintain propulsion, and even Max seemed surprised, pumping his head vigorously to gain speed. But to no avail. Head bowed, Max finished two lengths behind Mister Parker. Nicky Bianco, a victor in his first Templeton Million, kissed the sky with his whip. Head down Max passed his rival in the victory circle.

Back in the stable, Steven felt Max's hoof. Max reacted as if he had been stabbed.

"He almost won with a bad leg. What an incredible animal."

And with that Steven decided to give himself and his prize horse a month off.

Maybe I'll take Sophia to Disney World.

The next day Steven found himself with a relaxed Max at his stall and a smiling David Moriarty standing nearby.

"Sorry we couldn't win it for you boss," said Steven.

"Well, I'm happy Max is okay. I should have listened to you and scratched him. Go, enjoy the time with your daughter. You deserve it."

Just then this upbeat meeting was interrupted. Two grim long coated individuals, looking out of place, flashed something in gold. "Are you Steven Ricci?"

"Yes, that's me."

"We are State Police detectives. You are under arrest."

"Arrest? For what?"

"For the sexual abuse of your daughter, Sophia Ricci."

Chapter 15: The Trial

AS STEVEN WAS BEING LED OUT of the shed row David Moriarty sputtered, "I'll have my attorney post bail Steven." Even the horses' heads picked up at the cessation of all backstretch mania as a handcuffed Steven, head down, was guided out of the track.

At the police station Steven was given his Miranda rights, booked, and had his photo taken. "What am I being charged with?" said Steven, blinking repeatedly as if this movement would change the reality he was now in.

"Steven you have been charged with four counts of sexual misconduct; two counts of child molestation and two counts of sexual misconduct with a child under ten. Essentially the state is saying you abused your daughter on two separate occasions."

A quiet Steven was unable to respond, his tongue pounding his larynx.

The detective continued, a raised eyebrow eyeing Steven "Each one of these charges can result in five years in jail Steven. You have been read your Miranda rights. Do you want to say anything?"

Seeking to immediately curtail this living nightmare, Steven began, "Anything you want…"

Suddenly a bustling interruption; "He has nothing else to say," voiced a trim natty dressed redhead, wearing a bright blue bowtie. "Don't say another word Steven." Turning to the detectives he declared, "I'm his attorney gentlemen, Morris Stuart. I've already posted bail of $50,000. Steven gather your things. We are out of here."

"See you at the arraignment gentlemen," uttered the well-bred barrister as he ushered Steven out of the room.

Steven soon found himself in the cultivated offices of Morris Stuart and Associates. In that precise blue-blood language Attorney Stuart invited Steven into his dark paneled office, half of which was occupied by a large mahogany desk.

"Helen, get me all the records in this Ricci matter – doctors' records, protective service reports, and police interviews – everything you can find."

As the lawyer spoke, Steven surveyed the office. He saw framed degrees covering one of the walls – Georgetown, Harvard Law, and Law Review. Taking it all in Steven immediately sensed that this attorney might be great for a tax issue, but maybe not for the gritty world of false sexual abuse charges.

With red/gray manicured hair sandwiched between a bald palate, the fifty something attorney reminded Steven of a banker who smiled only when he made money. "Good for Mr. Moriarty, but not for me," Steven thought.

Attorney Stuart quickly disabused Steven of these notions.

"I've heard you're a great father Steven. That's important to me. Nothing more important than your kids."

He proudly showed Steven a picture of his gorgeous wife and two sons, both in military uniforms. "My older son is an Army Ranger, just come back from Iraq. My younger son just entered Annapolis. Couldn't be prouder of them both."

"Steven we will have your arraignment in two weeks. I'll have more information for you when we meet again next week. You just go back to work for now okay?"

"I guess I can't see Sophia, right Mr. Stuart?"

"No, sorry Steven. But let me get to work. I've successfully defended many such cases. Okay?"

"Do you need a retainer?"

"All set Steven."

A week later, an exhausted Steven, sleepwalking through the worst week of his life, sat again in Attorney Stuart's grand office. A pile of papers sat on the attorney's desk. In a serious tone the attorney explained to Steven what he had found out.

"Let me give you the etiology of this case Steven. Sophia's pediatrician filed an initial complaint with state protective services. He observed redness in your daughter's vaginal area and diagnosed two urinary tract infections in her after visits with you. Your daughter told him her daddy touched her down there when she put on her pajamas. The doctor was mandated to file this report."

Peering over his glasses as these words were being read, Attorney Stuart observed his client's face go from crimson to tomato red.

"Can I have a glass of water, pl....ease?" jabbered Steven.

Sophia's words left him recalling the two episodes which fueled Sophia's reaction. Always nervous about changing Sophia for bed, he normally left her pajamas on her bed and came back after she was done. Even Steven knew this was silly, but something made him shy about seeing his daughter undressed. Maybe because he wasn't around for bedtime when she was a baby. Maybe guilt for having been a bad father. Maybe a latent fear that Nicky could set him up?

On this particular night Sophia called she was ready, but when Steven walked in, she was itchy "down there." A blushing Steven looked at some redness in the crotch area. The next day she was fine, and Steven forgot about the incident.

The following weekend visit, Sophia woke Steven up with her stuffed toy Max. "Can we watch television daddy?" she asked, as a smiling Steven lifted Sophia onto the bed. As he settled her into the bed beside him, she winced as his arm hit the front of her pajamas.

"Are you okay honey?" asked Steven.

"Nicky says you shouldn't touch me down there."

Steven faltered, not sure what to say or do, but he immediately got out of bed, and walked about the room for a minute.

"What's wrong daddy?"

"Nothing honey," he told her as he sat down on the bed beside her.

Steven soon put the incident out of his mind – until now, when he heard these chilling words without any context.

Attorney Stuart's eyes looked closely at his perspiring client. "So you never touched your daughter inappropriately down there?"

"No, never. This is all Nicky Bianco. He's setting me up. He's telling Sophia what to say. Don't you see?"

"Let's forget Nicky for a minute Steven. The problem here is that since Dr. Sheppard interviewed your daughter, she has been interviewed by a child protective service worker, a police detective, and another attorney called guardian ad litem, who is Sophia's own attorney for these legal proceedings. It's very common, especially if these examiners ask Sophia such leading questions that Sophia comes to believe the abuse is true. She may be asked to remember so many things by so many questions, that she shuts down. After all, she is only six. It's understandable."

"My poor daughter," said a recovering Steven, realizing he was not the real victim here. "So she might come to believe I did abuse her?"

"It's possible, if the professionals around her are not careful."

"Will she have to testify?"

"Yes," said Attorney Stuart, "Unless…

Steven interrupted, "Unless I plead guilty?"

"I could probably get you a plea deal where you won't serve time."

Steven did not hesitate, knowing the repercussions to his reputation, "No, never."

But in the succeeding months, while he awaited trial, Steven almost came to the feeling that he was guilty of something. He could not get rid of the notion that his brush against Sophia's groin area in bed was no accident. But he knew it wasn't intentional, so why was he so afraid to even see his daughter naked? Was there some monster in him that could come out at any time? He was confused by these streaming thoughts rolling around in his head. Eventually Steven confided these feelings to his attorney.

Attorney Stuart was now more of a father figure than a legal advisor to Steven.

"Steven, from what you shared you had no male figure in your life, so it was just you and your mom. Maybe it triggered some unconscious things, but let's be clear – you did not sexually abuse your daughter."

So conflicted was Steven that Attorney Stuart would not let his client take a polygraph. "These underlying ruminations of yours could result in a false positive."

As the trial date for four counts of sexual abuse approached, the District Attorney's office sought to settle the matter before the trial.

Steven's barrister briefed him, "They have a weak case Steven, and they know it. They will settle it for one count of solicitation of a minor. You will get no jail time, and three years of probation."

"But I will have a guilty charge against me. I'll lose my trainer's license."

"Yes, that's true, but you will spare your daughter from having to testify against you." In response to Steven's question as to what Attorney Stuart would do, he answered honestly, "I don't know Steven. I really don't. You will have to make that decision yourself."

After many sleepless nights Steven decided on self-preservation. He had already seen evidence of the repercussions of being an abuser. After the arraignment David Moriarty had "suggested" that Steven take some time off from training to concentrate on his legal problems. In fact the mogul had called up some young hot-shot trainer, who looked more like a wall street broker who had probably never mucked a stall in his life.

Also, Steven had no idea what poor Sophia might be experiencing or how she was being brainwashed. And the more he ruminated on the issue, his anger was displaced from Nicky to Alyssa. How could she let her daughter be subjected to this legal charade? Is she in cahoots with Nicky in planning this deception? How could she allow her daughter to bear witness again and again to these strangers? These questions and more tormented Steven each sleepless night, no matter what sleeping pill he took.

Another woman reappeared in his life – her appearance mirroring his childhood days when he had to be rescued by his mom. During his rise to national stardom, his relationship with Carole had grown more distant. Married to a fireman and now girthy "good ole boy" townie Duck, Carole was content to sip beer and gossip with the wives at their husbands' softball games. Steven couldn't stand Duck, who bragged about his heroics in the town little league at age twelve.

On infrequent visits home, if Steven brought up any pressures from his success, Carole would feign interest, "You'll be okay honey." She knew Steven always took care of Steven." No, Monday bowling nights, Tuesday cookouts, and Wednesday Elks bingo, seemed to satisfy Carol's simple life. Steven was actually happy for her, as even since his youth his mother seemed to be a casual observer rather than a participant in life.

But after her son's arrest, Carole seemed jolted by her sleepwalking life. "This is all my fault," she cried in his small spartan apartment, which he rarely occupied in his prior life. Her renewed interest and perceived sympathy for her son did not prevent the following question. "You didn't do it right?"

Naturally Steven went ballistic. "Go home to the high school star Ma. You were never really there for me. Maybe if you had married a good guy when I was a kid, I wouldn't be in this position."

Recognizing the absurdity of his reckless comment, Steven apologized, "I'm sorry Ma. You didn't deserve that. I never listened to anyone. It's not your fault. I do know one thing. Nicky Bianco is behind this whole thing. He must be controlling Alyssa."

Hearing this name, Carole put down her gin and tonic, and bit her lower lip, as she did in times of stress. "It is Nicky, Steven. This goes back to your father."

“What do you mean, this goes back to dad?”

“Steven, I can’t talk about this.”

“Ma, tell me, what about Nicky and my father?”

But Carole was already heading for the door. “I got to go home.”

Despite repeated calls to his mother in the next week, Steven got no call backs. Her fat fireman husband finally told Steven, “She’s out bowling Steven. She’ll call later.” But she never did.

With weeks to the trial Steven had no time to pursue this mystery. As the trial was about to commence, Attorney Stuart prepared Steven for what to expect. “Yes, Steven, Sophia will testify, but only with limited observers.”

He then explained, “When she testifies, she will be accompanied by her own attorney. Other than the attorneys, court personnel, and the jury, there will be no other members of the public present. The prosecution will present their case in the sequence of the alleged abuse reports – the pediatrician, the protective service worker, and the state police detective.”

“I want to testify.”

“Let’s see how it goes Steven. It opens you up to all kinds of things about your personal life.”

So, on the announced day a sweaty Steven Ricci, sporting an uncomfortable suit, surveyed the individuals who would decide his fate. At the same time, the jury of eight women and four men got their first glimpse of the handsome defendant. Steven deflected their persistent gaze, not sure how an innocent man is supposed to act.

The prosecutor pointed a finger at the defendant, "The State will prove that this defendant Steven Ricci molested his daughter on at least two occasions. We have medical evidence to support the claim as well as the words of his six-year-old daughter. In addition, we have the words of the minor's mother, Alyssa Bianco, the former wife of the defendant, who will testify to the personality changes in her child. Thank you."

Attorney Stuart, green bowtie high on his neck, rose slowly from his chair, removed his glasses, and minimizing the combative tenor of the prosecution spoke to the jury as if they were all old comrades.

"Ladies and gentleman of the jury, this man who never knew his own father, was determined to be a good dad. Even with all the success he has achieved as a nationally known horse trainer, he found time for his daughter. We will prove that he is either a victim of a witch hunt, or innocent events have been twisted to abhorrent acts, and planted in his daughter Sophia's mind by a succession of so-called experts."

After that opening, a dazed Steven watched as a parade of individuals supported the State's claim. Dr. James Sheppard, a kindly looking elderly pediatrician testified first.

"Yes," he said in response to the prosecutor, "Sophia had two vaginal infections that were observed in the month of November, following visits with her father, Mr. Ricci."

"How do vaginal infections occur in children of Sophia's age?"

"The two most common causes would be poor hygiene or some sort of inappropriate contact in the area."

"And would it be uncommon for two bacterial infections to occur twice in a row when the child was with her father?"

"Yes, I would say that is unusual, even concerning, especially combined with the child's comments."

"That's all," said the confident prosecutor, smiling as she walked past the jury.

Attorney Stuart, resplendent in his bright green bow tie, calmly approached the pediatrician as if meeting a good friend. "Did you observe any symptoms besides the redness in Sophia's vaginal area?"

"No."

"Did you see evidence of any abrasion in the area?"

"No."

"Did Sophia react with fright or anxiety when you examined her vaginal area?"

"No."

"And wouldn't you expect someone who had recent trauma in that area to react badly to your touching her there?"

"I suppose so."

"And isn't it possible that a six-year-old, upon wiping herself after a defecation, could accidently insert bacteria into that area herself?"

"Yes, it is possible."

"Thank you, Dr. Sheppard."

The jury then watched a videotape of Sophia being interviewed by a State social worker, Mrs. Elizabeth Matthews, following the report of Dr. Sheppard. In the videotape, Mrs. Matthews speaks with a relaxed Sophia, legs swinging nimbly from her oversized chair.

Mrs. Matthews began her questioning, "Hi Sophia, I'm here to ask you a few questions. Do you like visiting with your father?"

"Yes, I do. I really like watching cartoons with him in bed."

"Do you spend lots of time in bed with your father?"

"Yes, I bring Max with me."

"Who is Max?"

"My stuffed horse my daddy gave me."

"Do you have your clothes on when you are in bed with dad?"

"Yeah, my P.J.'s.

"Sophia, does your dad ever touch you where you don't want him to?"

"Only when he tickles me."

"Have you ever told your dad to stop tickling you?"

"Yes, when I was sore down there. It hurt when I laughed, and I told daddy to stop tickling me."

"Did your dad stop?"

"Yes… Then he wanted to look at me, and he looked under my P.J.'s"

"Did your dad say anything?"

"He asked if anyone had ever touched me down there."

"And had anyone else ever touched you there?"

"No, but daddy looked at me there."

"And how long did your daddy look at you there?"

"I don't know. Pretty long."

"Like as long as a Disney song?"

Sophia raised her shoulders, "Yeah. I asked him to stop. I wanted to play with Max."

"Did your dad ever touch you?"

"I don't know." But then she added amiably, "I was putting on my P.J.'s one night and he kept looking at me down there and touched me."

"Did you ask him to stop touching you?"

"Yeah, I wanted to play."

"And did he touch you that night when you were putting on your pajamas?"

"I'm not sure."

"Sophie, think a little more about that time. Did he touch you?"

"I don't remember," said a solemn Sophia as she bit her fingernails.

"Did your dad put your panties on that night?"

"Yeah, I think so. I don't know."

Sophia raised her shoulders up and down again.

"I don't want to talk about it anymore."

During her testimony at the trial Mrs. Matthews confirmed that she had been a protective service worker for one year. Fresh out of college, this was her second sexual abuse investigation. On cross examination Attorney Stuart challenged Mrs. Matthews substantiation of the abuse allegations.

"Isn't it possible that this was a father concerned about his daughter's infections?"

"I don't believe so. She asked him to stop looking and touching her in her vaginal area."

"So you are saying he should have ignored the infection?"

"He should have brought it to the mother's attention. She is the custodial parent."

During Sophia's subsequent interview with the state police detective Denise Everett, a more damaging testimony against Steven was elicited. Again on videotape, Sophia seemed much more tense, gripping tightly to the arms of her chair. After several intense exchanges with the detective, Sophia looked around the room as if wanting to escape.

Staring solemnly at Sophia, Detective Everett asked, "Isn't it true Sophia that your dad looked at your pee pee every time he got you ready for bed?"

"I don't know. Yeah."

"And that made you feel icky, right?"

"Yeah."

"And when he touched you there, you asked him to stop?"

"Yeah."

Steven had to admit that in his quest to determine if Nicky was abusing Sophia he had focused more on her private areas in recent visits. Especially as he saw redness, he was present more when Sophia changed into her pajamas in the evenings. This concerned change was now being twisted and portraying him as a monster. Attorney Stuart admonished Steven, "You should have told me about this earlier Steven."

The prosecution then called Alyssa Bianco to the stand. The mother of a new son, Damien, now six months old, Alyssa looked tired and worn-out after a difficult pregnancy. She testified that prior to the cessation of visits Sophia had stopped looking forward to seeing her father. Her daughter told her, "Daddy's always looking at me when I change at night." She also told her mother that, "Visits are not fun anymore."

On cross examination Alyssa denied Attorney Stuart's suggestion that her difficult pregnancy allowed her husband more access to the child.

"No, I always bathed Sophia and put her to bed. I was not on complete bedrest."

She admitted, however, "No my husband does not like Steven, but he never badmouths him in front of Sophia."

Attorney Stuart called several witnesses to the stand who vouched for Steven's commitment to Sophia, including his mother Carole, David Moriarty, and other backside workers. The most dramatic part of the trial came when Attorney Stuart called Nicky Bianco to the stand. The trim jockey uncharacteristic in a three piece suit rather than silks pounced confidently to the stand, ignoring Steven's glare.

Attorney Stuart began the questioning. "Isn't it true that you have a long history with Steven Ricci?"

"Yeah. We knew each other as kids. Got into some bad stuff. We both grew up."

"And isn't it true that you harbored a grudge against my client for years. Especially when he took your then girlfriend Alyssa away from you?"

Nicky turned and smiled at the jury, "I guess it all worked out."

"And isn't it true that you have influenced Sophia to say these bad things against her father?"

"You heard her tell people what her father did. I had nothing to do with it."

"Have you ever bathed Sophia Mr. Bianco?"

"No, never. You heard my wife."

Similar accusations and denials went back and forth until the successful jockey left the stand. He gave a brief, triumphant glare at his nemesis. The climax of the trial occurred when the courtroom was cleared of observers, and Sophia entered the room. Dressed in a ruby red dress with ruffles flowing from the hem, she walked hand in hand with her attorney, Sandra Pierce. Eyeing her dad sitting up front with his attorney, Sophia broke free of the guardian's hand and ran excitedly to her father. The jurors watched as she landed in her father's arms saying, "Daddy, daddy." By fatherly instinct Steven just inhaled the scent of his daughter, while gripping her tight.

The judge said firmly, "Sophia can you sit in this chair next to me."

"Yes," she nodded, still grinning.

Attorney Pierce took a chair just beside Sophia, holding her hand. Co-counsel for the district attorney's office, a young woman, Julia Frost, who looked fresh from law school commenced the questioning.

"Do you like visiting with your dad, Sophia?"

"Yes. I miss going there with Max."

"Did you ever feel bad when you went there?"

"Yeah, sometimes my daddy touched me and asked a lot of questions."

"When you say touched me, do you mean in the area that you pee?"

"Yes."

"Have you ever asked him to stop touching you there?"

"I think so."

After a few similar exchanges Attorney Stuart cross examined Sophia, as a kindly father, which he was.

"Isn't it true that you miss your daddy Sophia?"

"Yeah, me and Max like watching cartoons with him."

"And when your dad changed you into your P.J.'s did he ever hurt you?"

"No. I just got tired of him asking me if I was okay down there."

"Sophia, did your dad ever touch you there when he was not changing you into your P.J.'s?"

Sophia, a bit nervous, looks at Attorney Pierce, who nods kindly. Sophia continues, "Yeah, one time he tickled me down there."

"When you say tickled, was it just there?"

Sophia relaxed a bit, "Oh no. He tickles me all over. It's fun."

Attorney Stuart, smiles and says, "Last question Sophia. Has your Mama's husband Nicky Bianco ever given you a bath?"

Her guardian Attorney Pierce objected to the question. "Sophia has denied this in the past. I don't think this question is necessary."

The judge overruled the objection.

Again Attorney Stuart asked, "Has Nicky Bianco ever given you a bath?"

Sophia, head bowed, answered, "I think so. Maybe once."

"Has Nicky Bianco ever told you to say bad things about your father?"

Sophia looked in her father's direction, "I don't know. He doesn't like my daddy."

Attorney Stuart called up Alyssa and her husband Nicky on redirect once more who both promptly denied Sophia's new claim. Alyssa firmly told the jury, "I was present for all bathing, and changing of Sophia for bed."

Nicky reaffirmed, "I never even mention Steven Ricci's name in my house."

And as the murky legal case went to the jury, Steven clearly realized one thing. He loved his brave little girl more than he could ever imagine. He was now in the jury's hands, wondering how they would consider his love for his child. For three days Steven sat at home waiting for the jury to come to a decision. He ruminated on this fact – that the jury saw how much my daughter loved me. They can't possibly convict me of hurting her, can they?"

On the fourth day Attorney Stuart told Steven to appcar in the Courthouse. The jury did not reach a verdict. No, they told the judge they were hopelessly deadlocked. The judge said he admired their efforts, but, "Your duty requires you to resume deliberations."

On the sixth day the weary, grim faced jury marched into the courtroom to declare they had reached a verdict. The tense courtroom was filled with family, horse folks, and media. Noticeably absent was David Moriarty. All present looked at the jury as its spokesman declared the verdict.

Chapter 16: Imprisonment and Beyond

LAYING IN HIS PRISON CELL Steven had plenty of time to digest the events that occurred that day. As the clerk told Steven to rise, he somehow did, but without feeling anything in his legs. He heard "not guilty" three times, and his heart soared. *The jury saw how much Sophia loved me,* he thought to himself. But then the last charge was read, "Guilty of one count of second degree sexual misconduct of a child under ten." Steven collapsed into his seat. Attorney Stuart had to usher him to his feet. He did not hear the judge admonish him for violating his daughter's trust, but he did hear the sentence. "One year in jail, followed by three years of probation." As the Court officers placed handcuffs around Steven's hands, Attorney Stuart whispered, "This is a miscarriage of justice Steven. We will appeal." Later Attorney Stuart polled the jury. He told Steven, "They only struggled with the infections on your daughter."

In his cell, waiting to be processed, Steven heard a beefy guard murmur, "They don't like didlers up at Lennox." And that's when Steven learned he would be serving his sentence up north, near the Ohio border. Lennox, a forbidden place where Steven had often driven by when he trained horses in nearby Covington. The large structure had always seemed so out of place in the bucolic rolling hills of blue grass country. The prison resembled an ancient fortress with weathered stone walls and guard towers instead of turrets. Layers of razor wire replaced moats and drawbridges.

Attorney Stuart spoke to Steven in the days before his transfer, "With good behavior you will be out in six months. Lennox is a medium security prison. I'll try to get you in a minimum-security campus facility here in Lexington." After hesitating for a moment the lawyer added, "If you want Steven, I can get you into the sexual offender unit at Lennox…"

Steven shouted a resounding, "No!" even before his attorney finished the sentence. "I would never go to such a place. I never did anything wrong. I'll take my chances anywhere else. I know you're going to tell me I'm in danger as a convicted abuser. But I'll take my chances."

Nodding, Attorney Stuart soberly shook Steven's hand as if it was their last time together.

When Steven received his dinner in his cell the first night at Lennox he saw that it was laced with sputum. He looked up to a smirking guard who ignored his request for a new meal.

At roll call the next morning Steven's long haired neighbor bared several missing teeth as he mouthed "lover boy," to Steven. At this point Steven quickly realized news of his conviction had spread rapidly in this confined world. Sitting alone with his powdered eggs and burnt toast Steven was joined by a diminutive prisoner, the deep crevices on his face tattoos of a life lived hard.

"You don't remember me, do you Steven? You used to let me exercise some of the horses in the morning."

Steven could not believe the aged hawk-like face was once one of the top jockeys at Templeton. When Steven first started mucking stalls, this jockey Sean Mazzuco hung around the backside looking for mounts. His reputation of putting anything in his mouth that was illegal had made him a racing pariah, and eventually a shell of his former self.

"Yeah, I screwed up my life Steven, but I'm sober now. Going on three years."

"How'd you end up here?"

Sean, speaking in a perpetual hoarse voice, the remnant of his drug days, spit out, "Out of it on meth for three days, my bud and I tried to rob our drug dealer. My bud stabbed the guy to death. We were both convicted of murder. Got another fifteen years before I can be paroled."

Sean quickly gave Steven an education on prison culture. "The guards are worse than the prisoners. They hate their life and do anything to stir up trouble. And I can get more meth from them than I ever got on the street. That's why I'm proud of my sobriety. Getting a three year sobriety chip next month. The guards, they told everyone about you and your daughter."

Steven interrupted him, "I never touched my daughter Sean."

"Doesn't matter Steve. I believe you, but someone's gonna get you. Either a shive or worse. That's how it is."

Steven knew what was worse – a sexual assault on a pervert was just prison justice. Steven knew he had to do something, and with Sean's help he soon developed a plan.

Sean croaked, "You will be out of here in six to nine months no matter what you do. Best thing is to go into the isolation unit. Locked up twenty-three hours a day."

"Sounds good," said Steven. "How do I get in?"

Days later Steven went into the exercise yard. Approaching the "meanest looking skinhead" on Sean's advice, Steven confronted the man. This boulder like prisoner with tattoos covering every part of his face stood firm, "What do you want sweetheart?"

Steven stared at this thick necked ball of muscle and declared, "You're using my weights."

Thick biceps reigned on Steven who did his best to avoid injury as the crowd urged the skinhead on. The badly beaten inmate might not have lasted the sixth minute, but fortunately the guards arrived in five. Steven was moved to the isolation unit.

Steven's tenure in isolation led to a psychological descent that only a "special" person would understand. His cell was now so small that arms outstretched, Steven could almost touch its faded lime walls. A toilet and sink were squeezed in, only inches away from his bed. As he sat on the edge of the snot encrusted, rusty cot covered with a pencil thin mattress, Steven blamed the world for his predicament.

His thoughts evolved…… *This is all Nicky's fault, became Lyssa had to be a part of this, to I hate my daughter.* His one hour of exercise per day allowed him to look at the sky and angrily proclaim, "You did this to me God!"

Eventually this blame game seemed to take all the energy from Steven's body. He barely picked at the cold oatmeal, stone like chicken fingers and cardboard like whipped potatoes slipped under his door three times a day.

With little energy for life itself, Steven allowed blonde sagebrush whiskers to grow wild on his face. Even the guards making their forced checks encouraged him to bathe. "You smell like shit Ricci."

But Steven did not care since the world did not deserve him. After several weeks of blame there was only one way out. Sitting on his bed Steven laughed, "They even removed the door frame so I can't end it there." Twisting and untwisting his bed sheets Steven glanced down at the four posts keeping his cot six inches from the smelly floor. "If I lean the bed against the wall I might be able to tie a sheet"...

But Steven had another problem. "The ceilings are barely seven feet high, so how can I gain momentum to hang myself?" His answer was in the cracked sink inches from his nose. "Soap!" He would layer soap under his feet, and slide down. With anger in his heart rather than fear Steven vowed, "I'll leave this crappy world tomorrow."

That night Steven had a nebulous dream that woke him. Able to wash his face by leaning forward six inches he glanced in the cracked mirror. He ruefully laughed, "I will look like a shit lime green corpse when they find me tomorrow." Asleep again Steven's dreams returned and grew more powerful. His daughter appeared in a blue skirt and ankle socks, sitting on the witness stand, her legs swinging from the oversized chair. But she is not testifying against him. No, she says in a firm voice, "Daddy, stop being angry at the world." Her repeated words grow louder and louder in Steven's dream until he begged her to stop. Covered in sweat, Steven awakens with his hands over his ears.

He cradles the knotted sheets and soap, his utensils of death. Sophia's words have somehow penetrated a walnut tight mind that sees the world only one way – his way. He begins to think about his poor daughter. *I wonder what she is doing right this second? I wonder what she thinks of me?*

Eventually Sophia's absence from him triggered memories of a father he never knew. One that Steven did not care to know. He had to confront that fact. *Why was I scared to learn about my father? Was it that learning about him would create pain in my life?*

And so it went in that difficult morning for this egotist. Steven thought about his relationships one by one – his mother, Alyssa, Pops, his friends, and realized that Sophia was right. He hid behind his fears of loss – his grieving – by using people. Anger replaced vulnerability. Steven cried for the first time in years. He got on his knees repeating the only words he retained from youthful Bible class. "Do unto others as you would have them do unto you."

In the days that followed, changes in Steven were imperceptible to others, but he had changed.

He thanked his jailers for his meals, and escorts to his one hour outside in the fresh air. Hair combed and freshly shaven, Steven no longer yelled at God. No he grew to thank Him for giving Steven another chance to right his wrongs. Hopefully to be a better father and son, and for once learn more about his own dad so he could come to terms with his death.

Two months later a new Steven received his first gift. He would be released immediately and serve the remainder of his sentence in a halfway house outside of Lexington. He would have to wear an ankle bracelet, work, pay rent and meet regularly with a probation officer.

As Steven walked out of what he once considered a decayed pit he now viewed Lennox as the site of his Baptism. He knew the vows he had made would be severely tested. *Promises in prison are easy. How will I react when things do not go my way?*

The halfway house was in a bedroom community ten miles east of Lexington named Everett. Steven occupied his own room in the sparce shot-gun ranch home that served as his new residence. Seven others lodged in three bedrooms that lined each tight corridor behind a front to back living and kitchen area. All rooms were endowed with several pieces of Salvation Army furniture that looked ready to collapse with the deposit of a heavy derriere.

The home's director, Sam Matthews, was a tall bespeckled man with downturned lips so tight his teeth disappeared. He laid down the rules of the home in a business-like tone, "If you follow the rules here Mr. Ricci, you will have no problems. Look at this chart for your weekly duties -trash removal, house cleaning, etc. You are expected to get a job within seven days and pay a weekly rent of $25."

Steven interrupted the staccato-like presentation of the director, "How do I find a job?"

Peering out over his glasses Mr. Matthews responded, "That's your problem. We have job listings on the message board in the dining room. As a level 3 sexual predator you cannot be within one half mile of a school."

As if prepared for Steven's "How…" response Mr. Matthews removed his glasses and sighed, "Look Mr. Ricci the other residents do not like your type here. You will have your own room because your would-be roommate Ray chose to move into another bedroom. In fact, the residents have told me they don't want you to cook for them. I'm not making a judgement about you Mr. Ricci, but the reality is people don't like sexual predators."

Steven simply said, "I see."

Seeming to take pity on Steven the director said, "Godfried's Supermarket is always looking for baggers. It's also far away from any schools."

The next day Steven took a bus and traveled to Lexington to meet his probation officer Deanna Williams. An overweight, middle-aged woman she hovered over a desk covered with folders and papers. Her large torso was supported by two sizeable arms protectively covering her desk. Without looking up from her paperwork Ms. Williams laid down the conditions.

"You have been assigned to probation with me for the next three years. I will meet with you twice monthly Mr. Ricci. I will also monitor your progress in the sexual offender group that you will attend here in Lexington."

Steven tried to intervene, "But I didn't offend...."

He was halted by a large hand which Ms. Williams held up in Steven's face. Her short brown hair cut high above her ears was contrasted by large ringlets that collapsed over her eyes. She often blew it out of her eyes.

"Don't give me excuses Mr. Ricci. You have been convicted by your peers. My job is to assess your risk to the community. I also want you to know I can continue your probation indefinitely if you don't cooperate with me or attend the offender group. If not, I can petition for you to return to prison. Is this clear? Now, here's your appointment card for the sexual offender group. See you in two weeks."

Steven soon attended his first male sexual offender group session. Of the twelve members, three had been convicted of rape or assault on an adult woman. Nine had sex with underage women from 15 to 17. Only one other man named Carl had been convicted of child sexual abuse on his own daughter. The group counselor Lidia Russo began each session the same way. Each member had to introduce himself and admit how they had hurt someone sexually. Beyond that Lidia allowed members to confront each other about denial or minimization of their acts.

The introductions began, but the atmosphere shifted when the counselor directed her attention to Carl, who was sitting next to Steven. "Last week Carl, you almost sounded like your daughter enjoyed your touching her."

A diminutive man, barely 120 pounds hunched nervously over his chair. To Steven he looked like the small beach seagull who hopes to salvage one chip from his stronger peers.

"I didn't mean it like that. It's just that she never said that it bothered her. I know it was wrong, but...but it was almost like a special thing between us."

The group murmured, and many shook their heads, but one large man got out of his chair. "You piece of shit. You think your daughter liked being raped!"

He unleashed more verbal barrage from the group. One was more compassionate, "Carl how could you say that. You make it sound like she liked it."

"You're right. I'm sorry."

To which the loud mouth retorted, "You disgust me Carl."

Counselor Russo interjected, "Peter you are angry. Sit down. It's important to remember Carl was a victim of sexual abuse himself. We all have to learn here that our behavior caused pain in others. You all took advantage of others and some of you used violence to achieve it."

Ms. Russo then turned her attention to the newest member. Why don't you introduce yourself Steven and tell us what you were convicted for."

"My name is Steven Ricci. I was convicted of molesting my six-year-old daughter, but I didn't do it."

The group members almost jumped from their chairs to confront this denier. The loud member of the group, Peter, shouted, "Don't pull that bullshit here. We won't allow it. Tell us what happened."

Steven hesitantly told his story: His rise as a horse trainer, the birth of his daughter, and the subsequent divorce, including the role of Nicky Bianco's setup. One member spoke up, "I remember you. I lost money on the white horse."

Ms. Russo restored order. "Look Steven, an independent jury of your peers listened to your story and didn't buy it."

Steven tried to explain the hung jury aspect, but Peter interjected, "Look, my friend you're not a rich horseman now. You won't become anything until you stop excusing yourself. Admit you did something wrong with your daughter."

Face crimson red Steven became silent as another member yelled out, "You're worse than Carl. At least he admitted he's an asshole."

After several weeks of continued denials, Steven was ignored by the group. Occasionally his name was uttered in group confrontations. "Why don't you sit next to Steven and avoid the truth."

One night Steven helped put away the chairs after another session of being the invisible group member. Group leader Ms. Russo sat Steven down. "Look, your probation officer Deanna Williams can keep you on probation indefinitely Steven, if you keep up this denial. You know I must send her monthly reports."

Steven responded, "Ms. Russo, I'll be the first person to tell you I was a bad person in my earlier life. Used everyone. Made excuses. Poor father. But this experience has made me a better person. Every morning I get on my knees and thank God for giving me another day to be better. My first goal is to rebuild my relationship with my daughter. I would never even look at her again if I was guilty of this crime. That's all I can say."

Ms. Russo responded, "I've met many people like you Mr. Ricci. You have to come to terms with your life. If you admit your offenses, life will get easier for you here."

"I can't admit to something I did not do Ms. Russo."

This message got to Probation Officer Williams during her routine fifteen minute session with Steven. With no eye contact she admonished, "I hear you are the only member of the offender group who will not participate. I have to remind you of the terms of your probation."

"I know Ms. Williams. But I cannot admit…"

Ms. Williams raised her hands from her protected desk. Dandruff flew from the curls of hair as she whistled it from her face. "See you in two weeks Mr. Ricci. You will be on probation indefinitely. I'm even tempted to revoke your probation for non-compliance.

One positive event occurred in Steven's sad life. Six weeks of bagging groceries at Godfried's Market had made Steven a popular man. Greeting the familiar faces with a smile, he would chat up the customers. "Good morning Mrs. Carmody, let me take those bags out to the car for you." "How's the leg doing Mr. Fitch?" His appreciative boss gave Steven a dollar raise.

That all changed one afternoon. A woman who always had a ready smile for Steven became venomous. As Steven reached to bag one of her purchases, she spat, "Don't you touch my groceries, you pervert." She spoke so loudly that Steven's manager ran over.

"Do you hire perverts here at Godfried's? I saw this…this child abuser's picture at the post office."

"Please, Mrs. Griffin, keep your voice down," whispered the nervous manager. "Steven maybe you should go home for the day."

Head down Steven felt the once friendly eyes of customers and co-workers reigning incredulously as they followed him to the exit.

Steven pulled his baseball cap down over his head on the bus ride home. He wished it could cover his whole body and make it disappear. To Steven the bus driver's "Have a good day," greeting as he exited the bus was, "Have a good day, you pervert."

Steven got on his knees in his solitary room at the halfway house. "Please God, help me. I'm not sure I have the strength to go on." He sobbed and sobbed until his head hurt. Try as he might to quell them, suicide thoughts again grew louder in his brain. "No one would even miss me."

A despondent Steven climbed into bed to be met by God rather than Sophia. In this dream God told him many of His saints were strengthened in their darkest hour.

The Lord spoke, “This pain in your darkest hour Steven is your test. Believe in Me and life will get better.”

That morning Steven awoke and found the nearest church. For some reason his legs felt light, so light he felt glad to be alive. Regular Mass became part of Steven’s life, once he found a church not close to a school.

The next day after his morning prayers, Steven showered, dressed in his best, and went looking for work. His manager at Godfried’s said he would mail Steven his last check. A block from the halfway house was a dry cleaner Steven had often walked past. “Sal’s” proprietor was a loud, boisterous redhead, who would often shout out hellos to passersby as he pressed clothes. As Steven slowly walked by Sal’s, the redhead yelled, “Hey kid, come in here. Want to play some cards?”

Sal was known in the community as a fun loving character who called everyone kid. He had no strangers in his life. A bachelor, he considered everyone his family. He was good-hearted, and gave generously to every charity group who asked. Sometimes he might come to an event in a “borrowed” suit he had just dry cleaned. The community loved this zany fortyish guy, who wore Bermuda shorts in the winter just for fun. Many a smiling dry cleaning customer lost a game of gin rummy to this crazy clothes cleaner.

On this particular day Steven later remembered that God seemed to send another angel at his most needy time.

"Why so sad kid? Want to play some gin rummy?"

"Don't really know how to play. I've been in the racehorse business most of my life. Never really played cards."

"What's your name kid?"

"Steven Ricci."

Sal let out a belly laugh, his long red hair flopping over his forehead. "You know how much money I've lost on your horses?"

Steven offered, "I didn't lose them all Sal. I won nearly 30% every year."

"Well," said Sal, "I must have had the other 70%. Sit down. I'll pour you a coffee. So you're looking for work huh kid?"

"Yeah, but you should know I'm a level three sexual offender. It might hurt your business explaining the incident at the grocery store."

"Let me worry about the public. They flow where the breeze is going, and ugly news travels like a hurricane." Then for the first time Sal's face grew serious. "Tell me what happened."

And for the next hour this funny looking redhead who wore loud Bermuda shorts in the dead of January just because, studied Steven carefully.

After Steven concluded his story, Sal said, "I'm convinced you're okay kid. When can you start? That nasty woman from Godfried's makes a scene here and I'll throw her out. You deserve a chance kid, and I'm the boss here."

And with that the new friends shook hands. The new Steven slowly accrued people who believed in him. He would never forget these lifesavers -some day he would be a raft for others.

Chapter 17: A New Steven

FOR THE NEXT YEAR STEVEN came under the spell of Sal and Sal's zany life. Working hard six days a week, Steven could hand press any oxford shirt in two minutes without damaging a button. Sal would host weekly poker games in the backroom, as participants passed bourbon back and forth. Invariably Sal would win. Steven suspected that Sal did not drink the bourbon like his partners. But as they departed, even with pockets bereft, the losing players would hug Sal, simply because he was so much fun to be around. Madcap Everett stories about Sal winning a goldfish eating contest brought memories of happier carefree days back to his friends.

Sal served as Steven's Uber driver to his probation officer meetings and shared with Sal what transpired in those meetings. Between puffs of the cigarettes Sal hand rolled each morning Sal exhorted, "I hate people who do their jobs without any heart. Why the hell did they get into that line of work."

Dreading both events Steven simply said, "I know."

"Don't worry kid, it's too much paperwork for her." Sal laughed, "Hey don't get any dandruff in the car."

Speaking of cars Steven was perplexed that Sal always drove old beat up cars with dents everywhere. In fact he had three of them. Steven never knew which squeaky door he was to open for the ten mile drive to Lexington.

One day he piped up, “Sal, why don’t you trade these cars in and get one good car?”

“Are you kidding. I got it made. Anyone can hit me and I don’t have to worry about it.”

Steven saw the wisdom of this crazy logic one day. A furious Sal watched as a car broke into a funeral procession. Sal always made a sign of the cross when he witnessed this sacred event. Sal ran his car into this interloper’s bright red convertible. The stunned driver, practically in tears, stammered, “You hit me on purpose!”

“That’s right.” Then throwing his Sal’s Cleaners card at the disabled car he said, “Sue me.”

In his second year at Sal’s, Steven came to believe that this crazy red- head had saved his life. He even attended daily Mass with this human anachronism, who entered church after taking his first shot of bourbon.

“I’ve been in jail before kid. Don’t worry. God won’t send you back.”

One sultry day Steven’s sweat poured onto oxford shirts he had just steam cleaned. He commented, “I think the air is warmer than the dryers Sal.”

Sal was too busy laying down his cards. “That is gin Charlie. You owe me $40.”

Charlie grinned, “You’re one lucky guy Sal,” as he turned over a double sawbuck.

Steven's laughter was interrupted by a phone call from his attorney. Steven then heard the magic words from a jubilant Morris Stuart. "Steven the appeals court ruled in our favor. They said your daughter's testimony was a testament to faulty interview techniques. I just spoke to the prosecutor's office. They will not recharge you. In fact, they could not recharge you given the language of the Appeals Court. You are a free man."

"You mean no more probation officer or offender visits?"

"That's right. As of today you have no record. You can live and work wherever you want."

Overhearing the conversation Sal poured three glasses of bourbon. "It's time to celebrate kid."

Now completely free, the new Steven had to consider his options. Should he go to Court to try to see Sophia? He was so far out of the racing loop that he didn't know where Alyssa and Nicky were living. He considered that Sophia was now nine years old, and her half-brother Damien was almost three. No, the wounds were too fresh. And then he didn't want to upset Sophia anymore. No, he would wait a few years until Sophia was old enough to digest the ugliness of thc Court stuff.

So he decided to write her a letter at her last known address to tell her how much he loved her. The trash barrel was soon filled with yellow lined pages of various lengths. Some were long, tortuous love letters, where he assured his daughter he never blamed her for his imprisonment, and she shouldn't feel any guilt herself. Instead, he opted for a simple, "I love you. I hope you're well. I'll see you soon."

The second consideration of his freedom was his own future. Did he want to reapply for a horse racing license? Did he want to get out of the miserable State of Kentucky? Maybe a fresh start in the sunshine of California? After careful consideration, Steven decided to stay right where he was.

Now a regular member of Sal's "rat pack" gang of poker players, he simply felt a freedom unlike ever before. Steven now opened up with his new friends, telling them about his better days in horseracing.

"Steven, tell us about Rumi Rose, so we can all remember her."

These poker friends admired Steven for his love of horses. And he valued the friendships he now had in Everett, where they had once hooted him out of Godfried's supermarket. Now patrons shook his hand when he shopped there.

At first this acceptance was because of the reputation Sal had in his hometown. "If you're a friend of Sal's ….." But over time, those same patrons who he once carried groceries for recognized he was a decent man. Steven could now do some other things he enjoyed, like assisting Sal in coaching Little League Baseball.

The nasty woman who once called him a pervert at Godfried's came to the dry cleaner's one day. "I want to apologize to you Steven." It helped that Sal called out the hypocrisy of his beloved community with his exclamations to everyone that, "Steven is a good man!"

When Steven informed Sal of his decision to stay put, Sal took out his bourbon and stated, "Let's play cards."

For the next year Steven was content pressing clothes at Sal's Cleaners. He also kept in close touch with his mom, whom he called often.

"I like this new Steven, honey."

He wrote more letters to Sophia, each in more depth, telling her how much he loved her. He never heard a response. His nightly dreams often centered on what Sophia's interests were, or what she might be learning in school. But his unconscious mind seemed to prevent him from pursuing her in "reality."

"It's better for her that I stay away. Some day she will know how much I loved her."

On a sweltering summer day at Sal's, perspiration rained down Steven's forehead as he pressed customers' clothing. Sal had left him as "manager" when Steven declined to go to the local racetrack with Sal and his cronies. As he reached for a jug of water at his side to cool his scorching head, he heard someone enter the shop. A haggard figure in a long trench coat shuffled through the door.

"Good afternoon, sir. Are you picking up?"

"Don't recognize me Steven?" croaked the stranger's voice.

Steven studied the pasty face and suddenly recognized something about the same playful azure eyes. "Pops! Is that you?"

"Yeah Steve, took me quite a bit to find you."

Steven ran from behind the counter and squeezed his old mentor. He could feel Pops's ribs underneath his trench coat.

"Pops, here sit down," said Steven as he guided his old friend to a chair.

"Thanks. I've been fighting this bone cancer for a while. It looks like it got its teeth into me good, just like Gal Gloria did to you, remember?"

Steven struggled to smile. The two talked for some time about things, and soon the memories, the good ones, brought each one to earlier days.

"Pops, where have you been all these years? No one heard from you."

"I got sick of all the bullshit with the racing business. Everyone used these beautiful animals for their own selfish needs. Rumi Rose's death was the final straw." Hesitating a moment Pops added, "By the way, I never held you responsible for her death. I would have done the same thing as you in my younger days. But I realized I loved those animals too much to put them in danger."

As he talked, Pops's lungs seemed to run out of air after each sentence. Steve gave Pops his jug of water and placed a cool compress on Pops's neck. Despite the heat Pops refused to take off his tired slicker.

Pops continued, "After I left Templeton I went out to Wyoming. I camped out near the wild Mustangs that roamed free, away from the tyranny of humans. These feral beasts, running free in their natural environment are a thing of beauty, Steven."

Steven, feeling a bit energized now by just visualizing this sight, replied, "It sounds beautiful Pops. I miss those magnificent animals too."

"I know what happened to you Steven, I've been keeping tabs on you."

"Pops, you know I didn't…"

Pops put his fingers to his lips stopping the conversation. "I know you love your daughter." And that was all that had to be said between the old friends.

"Steven, this is why I'm here. I can't watch those Mustangs in the desert forever. One night, sitting at a campfire in Wyoming, I got an idea. I decided to open a thoroughbred retirement farm for old racehorses. So I plunked my money down on a hundred acres of fertile land in the Snake River Valley. Most people think Wyoming is all desert and sage brush. Well, let me tell you, Steven, nothing beats this area. The hay and barley grow wild. My horses run free all day in the pasture, and drink from the Snake River when they get thirsty. I have over a hundred racehorses now, and they run only when they want to Steven. We even have a few arthritic Mustangs in separate stables."

"That is a wonderful thing Pops. Maybe I'll see it one day," Steven commented as he placed starch in some custom white shirts.

"Steven, look," said a serious Pops. "I've got maybe three months to live. I need someone to help take care of the place when I'm gone. I got a crackerjack manager, Juanita Sanchez. She loves those horses like we do, but she can't do it alone. We got adoption and retraining of these animals in addition to their day to day care. It's a big operation. You'll also be happy to know that my old assistant Owie has been helping me for the past year. But they need help, Steven, when I'm gone."

Steven smiled. He had often thought of how Owie was doing. "Pops, I don't know. That life brought me tremendous pain, and I'm a different person now. I'm really at peace with myself for the first time in my life."

"I can see that Steven. You are a changed man. A good man. But I do know that you love these animals, like I do. Please, at least just come out and see the operation for yourself."

With that, Pops slowly rose and gave Steven a pamphlet entitled, "Wilson's Horse Sanctuary."

Pops slowly shuffled toward the door. "Pops, where are you going now?" Steven called out.

"Back to Wyoming to die my friend."

Chapter 18: Snake River Days

THAT NIGHT SAL WAS IN a particularly giddy mood. “Hey Steven, I put $100 bucks on this 30 to 1 racehorse but he didn’t run a lick. The only reason I bet on him was he was a gray horse. I love grays.”

Steven immediately thought of his old friend Majestic Max. Steven told himself Sal would have put down $200 at the sight of the rare white horse.

“Sal, I had an old friend stop by today, Pops Wilson. He is the best racehorse trainer who ever lived. He understands horses better than anyone I have ever known. (Laughing) I think he loves these beautiful creatures more than people.”

Sal countered, “I think that applies to you, too, kid.”

“What do you mean?”

“You know when we have our card games, and the guys pepper you to tell them racehorse stories? That’s the only time I see you really happy Steven. It’s like cards for me kid. We all have our passions.”

Steven paused for a moment and then continued, “Well, Pops came to see me today. He’s dying Sal, and wants me to go out to Wyoming to help with a thoroughbred sanctuary for retired racehorses. I’m not sure what to do. I love my life here. I think living in Everett is the happiest I've ever been."

As he handed Steven a bourbon, Sal said, "Everett ain't going anywhere my friend. You can always come back. Your ass belongs around those beautiful animals."

While alcohol normally made Steven melancholy, accentuated by dreams of Sophia, today it did not. He thought to himself, Sal's right. I want to see these retired animals rewarded for all their hard work. If it doesn't work out, I can always come back.

A month later, after saying good-bye to Sal, and his poker friends, Steven was on his way to Wyoming. As his plane descended into the small airport near the Snake River, he felt transported to a new world. Cattle roamed free on

expansive prairies overlooked by rugged fingerlike mountains that appeared to reach for the sun. Vast grasslands swallowed the few homes that seemed only to taint the majestic landscapes created by God himself.

Once arrived, Steven was greeted by a smiling Owen, who gave his old friend a giant bearhug. Steven threw his small suitcase, containing the remnants of his new life, into the four wheel truck, and jumped in beside Owen. They soon pulled off the highway at a sign that said Roundtop Mountain.

Mesmerized by the passing landscapes Steven said, "Owie, are there any people around here?"

Owie responded, "I thought the same thing when I got here. We are a long way from Templeton. But you will love it here. We got a little town nearby that has a bank, a restaurant, and post office. There's even a little joint called Daisy's that has dancing on Saturday nights. But we got this beautiful land and over 100 happy horses bud. What could be better?"

As the speck of Roundtop Mountain grew larger, Owie shoved his bud, "Look over there Steven, at the Mustangs."

Steven marveled as about thirty compact wild animals with short legs, a variety of coat colors, and wild manes and tails paraded carefree in the extensive prairie before them.

"They are protected here by the government."

Steven muttered, "They look so happy."

As the mountain ambled closer to the traveling truck Steven asked, "How did you end up here Owie?"

"Things got rough for me when you left. Moriarty hired this hot shot trainer who treated racehorses like a bond fund. Everything was about blood lines and analytics. I tried to tell him that you have to be patient with horses -they all have personalities. But he was constantly telling Moriarty to buy and sell different horses. He formed no connection to our horses. Naturally, we butted heads – and he convinced Moriarty to fire me."

Owen continued, "I went to work for Caldwell for a while, but that didn't work out. He's an asshole. I hit the bottle hard and was back mucking stalls when Pops called me about a year ago. Now I'm one year sober. They even have AA meetings nearby."

The topic of Caldwell triggered the memory of Nicky Bianco, and naturally Alyssa and Sophia. Steven asked, "Does Bianco still ride for Caldwell?"

"I'm not sure Steven. I know he had a serious fall a few years back and was laid up a while. I wish I knew more about your daughter and Alyssa, but I've been off the grid for a bit."

"I know. I've been sending letters to my daughter at their old address in Lexington, and getting no response."

Soon the dirt road ended. In front of the two men was a miniature mountain, the son of towering peaks that framed panoramic vistas. Roundtop Mountain hosted foothills with ascending trees through which trails meandered, culminating at a rocky summit.

A sign welcomed visitors, "Welcome to Wilson's Horse Sanctuary. If you love these animals, you are welcome here." Steven smiled as he thought, *That's Pops."*

Fenced paddocks and pastures outlined the Snake River which scissored Pops's property. Steven marveled at Pops's creation - barns and stables sat beside feeding facilities and riding arenas. It was an oasis designed not for people, but for horses.

Owen ushered Steven into a sizeable home adjacent to the main paddock. The home's large veranda furnished with comfortable rocking chairs allowed for a spectacular view of all the man-made and natural wonders of the area. A hissing sound announced Steven's entrance to the living room, in which stood a large hospital bed. Its occupant stirred as a nurse adjusted higher oxygen levels for the patient's weak lungs.

The old man looked up and said, "Steven you made it."

Without his glasses on, Pops's face looked like white cauliflower with two dull blueberry eyes. Those eyes danced as Pops asked, "What do you think?"

"I think you created a heaven for these horses Pops. I can't believe how beautiful it is here."

"Good, good," Pops repeated between rough sips of air.

As Pops talked an olive complexion woman in horse gear took the nurse's notes from her. Dark hair pulled tight to her head accentuated expressive brown eyes above which sat thick brows. When the nurse left Pops introduced Steven to the facilities manager Juanita Sanchez. Without a smile, she shook Steven's hand firmly. Steven felt the coarse hand of someone who had raked plenty of hay.

"Pops, you have got to get some rest," said the Hispanic woman, affectionately. "The nurse increased your level of morphine to help with the pain."

As Pops tried to wrestle the oxygen tube away from his nose, Juanita intervened as if harnessing a horse.

"I can't talk to Steve with this thing in my nose," Pops said forcefully.

"I'm not kidding Mr. Wilson," retorted a stern Juanita, the only person who did not call him Pops.

"See Steven, I can't win. I've tole Juanita all about you. Just ignore her scowl. It takes her a while to like someone."

Then as Juanita ushered everyone out of the living room, a hint of a smile crossed her face. She turned to Pops, "Now you get some rest."

The three people sat on the veranda rocking chairs. Owen broke the silence, "Steven and I go way back Juanita. He can be a big help to us here. And I know that's what Pops wants."

As Owen spoke Steven felt Juanita's dark almond-shaped eyes viewing him with suspicion.

"As long as you know I'm in charge here, we will get along fine. Owie will help you get set up in the apartment near the stable. We have lots of things going on here -thoroughbred rehabilitation, riding lessons, tours, adoption, and more. I know you were a racehorse trainer, but this isn't horseracing. You have a lot to learn, okay?" said the no nonsense woman.

As she was about to leave, Juanita turned back. "The nurse told me Mr. Wilson has only a few days left. You better say your good-byes soon."

When Juanita was out of sight Steven said, "She's not very warm and fuzzy is she Owie?"

"She's quite a woman Steven. She's all business. This place would not exist if it didn't make money, and she makes it profitable. When she came here this place was hemorrhaging money. You know Pops loves horses, but he is not a businessman. When she came here four years ago, she turned the place around. And she loves Pops like a father. She is the only one who lives in the big house with Pops. He would have died two years ago without her."

The next morning at 5 a.m., while ornery horses were awaiting their breakfast, Steven was given his assignment for the day.

"I thought it best if you feed, wash and groom the horses since you know all about that," said "Sergeant Juanita", Steven's silent name for his new boss. The staff of five, aided by Snake River volunteers were given written assignments by the boss. Steven laughed at the irony as he thought, "Right where I began." But he soon realized how much he missed these snorting 1,000 pound roans.

After feeding and bathing the animals, Steven used a soft brush to clean and polish their coats. As he carefully untangled the horses manes and tails, sensitive areas where racehorses can react badly, he was surprised at how relaxed the horses remained. It was as if the retired animals knew their hard days on the racetrack were over. They could put a little girth on their belly and allow any person to clean them if they want. And they could also run whenever they wanted to.

By 10 a.m. the morning work was done. Steven and Owie went up to the big house to see Pops. The reclining figure, now a bag of bones seemed to have deteriorated overnight. It was as if Pops was waiting for Steven to appear before he let himself go. Eyes still closed, Pops wiggled his finger for Steven to come closer. Steven bent in close to Pops, and he whispered in Steven's ear.

Steven nodded his head, "I understand Pops."

A smile crossed the old man's face, and with Owen and Juanita holding each of his hands, the old man stopped breathing. Juanita, visibly shaken, placed her head on Pops's chest and murmured, "I love you Mr. Wilson."

Three weeks later Steven asked to ride the calmest pony on Wilson's Sanctuary. After all, he was a horse trainer, not an equestrian. On his lap sat a cardboard box containing Pops's ashes. Steven navigated the rugged landscapes, admiring the cloud covered sky, the sun peeping through, shining its warmth on plateaus and low basins all around him. Soon Steven found what he was looking for. A team of free-roaming Mustangs roared into sight led by a sturdy bay. The magnificent horse snorted in Steven's direction as if to say, "You're on my property." Steven released the ashes as the eight member horse family, embodying the freedom Pops desired, galloped out of sight.

Chapter 19: Steven's New Life

POPS HAD WHISPERED ONE OTHER THING to Steven on his deathbed. He told Steven he was leaving the Sanctuary to Juanita, but he hoped Steven and Owie would help her run it. In fact, when Pops's will was read, it stipulated that Steven and Owen would have a life estate on the Farm. They had a home there for as long as they lived.

One final thing Pops whispered to Steven, "I think you and Juanita would make a great couple." Steven thought Pops's death morphine had kicked in by then. Sure, she was attractive, but no one had ever seen her with her hair down, never mind in a dress. In fact, Steven called her a sergeant because she reminded him of other tough women he had seen in the backside. Many of these hard-luck women were lesbians. Some had been through very bad experiences with men. He wasn't sure if Juanita was a lesbian, but he was convinced she didn't like men. Many of the volunteers she recruited at the Sanctuary were women. When working with the women, Juanita seemed to be more relaxed and affable. Observing her, Steven had to admit on those rare smiling occasions, Juanita's sharp cheekbones and well-defined features gave her the regal look of a Spanish queen.

Following Pops's death, Juanita started a new tradition at the "big house," the large farmhouse she once shared with Pops. Juanita hosted meals every Saturday night for the staff and local volunteers. Steven and Owie would leave their solid, but modest dormitories attached to the stables on Saturday night after a hard week of work to attend these functions. Juanita turned out to be quite a good cook – empanadas, paella, and pupusas were her specialties. After dinner many of the crowd would head to Daisy's bar, one of only eight buildings in town. Local talent would provide the entertainment by simply signing a sheet at Daisy's. Consequently, the music ranged from hillbilly, and blues to rawhide like cowboy love songs.

Steven often declined to go to Daisy's. Although he knew he was now a better person, he still beat himself up whenever he thought of his daughter Sophia. He thought of her often but decided to stop writing to her.

She probably doesn't want to hear from or see me, he rationalized. His dream was that one day she would magically appear in his life, and everything would be fine.

On night, stomach full after another Saturday night feast, Steven and Owie shared Templeton remembrances on the veranda.

"I never met a gal like Rumi Rose, Steven," gushed Owen. "She was almost human, the way she understood what she needed to do on the racetrack."

Steven's eyes grew misty as he drained on his pipe, a habit he started after Pops's death.

"Her heart was too big for her body, Owie. I should never have let her run that day."

Silence enveloped the two friends as they admired the shades of orange, red, and blue desert sky, set ablaze by the setting sun.

Owie broke the silence, "Steve, come on down to Daisy's with me."

"Thanks, but I'm going to turn in early. The hungry horses won't know it's Sunday morning."

"Okay then, see ya," said Owen as he walked into the night.

As Steven got up to leave, the now diamond-like stars pierced the black sky. He heard the door slam. Juanita appeared, apron still wet from the last of the dishes. She asked, "Mind if I join you?"

Steven sat back down and answered, "I was just leaving, but it's hard to leave this celestial show."

Juanita gave a rare smile. "I love it here too. Pops and I would often sit in these chairs for hours. He would smoke his pipe in the same chair you're in."

Steven blushed, "I don't know why I picked up a pipe, but I'm sure Pops got something to do with it."

Gazing at silhouettes of mountains that resembled giant soldiers, Juanita said, "Pops told me a lot about you. He said you were his best student. He said that you were successful as a trainer because you understood the animals."

Steven smiled, "I don't know how to say it better Juanita, but the first time I saw a thoroughbred I felt better about myself. I liked them more than most people."

Juanita's eyes drifted as she responded, "I know what you mean."

As time went on Steven began to look forward to these Saturday night soirées. After spending twelve hours a day working hard all week, learning all facets of the operation, Steven figured he was allowed a bit of relaxation. Often, he even put on an apron after dinner to help Juanita with the dishes.

Steven quickly realized Juanita was as guarded about her past as he was. And beneath these blazing Saturday night desert shows, the two scarred individuals slowly opened up to each other.

"Even though I know I never touched my daughter, I felt guilty for something. It's weird, but I think it's related to being a bad husband and a bad father. Those days in solitary changed me, Juanita. I realized I was a very selfish person who really cared little for other people. Shit, I tormented little girls in the schoolyard when I was a kid just for fun."

Juanita smiled, "I'm glad I didn't go to your school."

As the months went by, Saturday night discussions between Juanita and Steven became more and more intimate. Still, Juanita would only share that she was forced to leave her house at the age of fifteen. A friend told her she could get a job in the horse stables, and that's where she first met Pops.

"I lied to Pops mainly because I needed a place to sleep."

Steven confessed his own runaway story to Juanita. "I wonder how many kids Pops helped like us," he said. Juanita laughed – not smiled- for the first time. As Steven studied her, he thought, "She's so much prettier when she laughs."

One Saturday night Juanita sat on the veranda with a surprise. She wore her hair down, and her thick, dark curls cascaded around her shoulders. The light from the stars reflected off her face, and Steven did a double take as her stern features now softened in the moonlight. Steven gazed at her almond eyes and full lips.

Juanita finally opened up to him, "I don't trust a lot of people Steven, especially men. But I think you should know my story. I ran away from my home because I almost killed my father. I was thirteen at the time. He had molested me since I was a child, and I couldn't take it anymore."

"Juanita, I'm so sorry."

"No one knows this, not even Pops."

Steven felt honored having been trusted with this information.

Juanita continued, "My parents were born in Puerto Rico. The man is king there. My mother was only sixteen when she married my father. He was twenty-one. My mother was one of fifteen kids, and her father basically gave her away to my dad, since he had a good job as a plasterer."

"They came to New York City where I was born. My twin sisters were born six years later. My mother had many miscarriages, and my father often berated her for not giving him a son. Eventually, my family moved to California when my dad's company relocated."

"My father was a bad man, Steven. He always yelled at my mother, calling her a pig or worse. He cheated on her with many women, and bragged to her about it. I think my poor mother was just beaten down. She started to drink, just like my father. When I was eight years old, I was changing my sisters' diapers before I left for school."

She hesitated, sipping in the cool desert air. "Anyway when my mother was passed out one day, my father came into my bedroom. I was seven at the time. He would touch me and say there was nothing wrong with it. When I said it hurt, he would slap me. To this day Steven I cannot drink alcohol, because the smell reminds me of my father's breath."

Steven moved closer to Juanita, as her tears welled up. Looking away from him to the mountain ranges, Juanita murmured, "It just got worse and worse. Thank God I didn't get pregnant."

Juanita, still turned away from Steven as if unable to face him, continued, "One night I heard my mother's footsteps at the door. In the hallway light I saw the darkness of her body intercept the light. I thought, Thank God. My mother is going to rescue me, and this will be over. Without any sound the light reappeared under the door as her shadow disappeared. That night I knew it would never end."

"As you can imagine Steven, this thing was the center of my life. I had no friends or outside activities. I took care of my sisters every day and dreaded when the nights came." The tears came as Juanita spoke softly, "I had no one to help me Steven."

Steven protectively took Juanita's hands into his.

Juanita needed to continue her story. "The last straw was when I saw my father looking at my sisters as he looked at me; not as a loving father, but as a possessor. One night as my father stumbled drunkenly into my bedroom and ordered, "Juanita, turn over," I turned and stabbed him in the chest with a steak knife. They say I missed his heart, where I was aiming, by two inches. I called 911, and the police came."

Steven spoke kindly to her, "Juanita, I'm so sorry for you." Suddenly Juanita pulled away and viewed him suspiciously. Had the secret she had buried so long been told to the right person, her eyes seemed to radiate. Steven seemed to understand, "Juanita, you can trust me. I never knew my father, but I'm lucky compared to you. I think we are both damaged souls, who survived all we've been through, and came away as better people. I'm so honored you shared this with me."

She allowed Steven to take her trembling hands, and both just sat there, neither saying a word for what seemed like hours.

Finally Steven broke the silence. "What happened after the stabbing?"

"My father recovered and went to jail. My sisters went to live with my father's mother in New York. She is actually a nice woman, with an asshole for a son. My sisters are beautiful young women, who graduate from high school this year. They are both going to college. I'll make sure of that. My mother died of cirrhosis of the liver a year later.

After spending two years in jail, my father scooted back to Puerto Rico and got himself another wife."

"Me? I went into a couple of different foster homes. I didn't feel welcome. I was treated like an outsider, never a member of the family. I didn't go to school much, and started hanging around with losers, since that is what I felt I deserved in life. I ran away from the last home when my foster father started looking at me the same way my father had."

Juanita looked deep into Steven's eyes as she said, "He wasn't interested in being father of the year, if you know what I mean."

That night marked a sharp distinction in their relationship. More weeks passed as the kindred companions shared their failures and hopes. Juanita had her own fears about the growing relationship, "I have to take us slow," she told Steven.

Steven identified with her fears, "Juanita, I have plenty of scars as you know. I have to prove I'm a better person to myself."

But trust eventually melted their mutual fears. Handholding led to hugs and kisses. The intimacy each craved was consummated in the big house months later with tears of pain and love. Somewhere in the desert sky Pops's cherub face was smiling.

As Steven's and Juanita's relationship was established, so was the true partnership of the horse sanctuary. The happy years went by quickly for the contented couple. Juanita ran the multiple programs with military precision and made them profitable. Steven mucked stalls, conducted tours of the Farm and did everything but ride the horses. After all, in his mind he was still a horse trainer.

Equestrian lessons became just a natural part of Juanita's business model. Children wanting a pony for their birthday could purchase a rescued one at the Sanctuary. Owen was promoted to Manager of the horse stables, furthering the public's willingness to interact with and care for these beautiful animals.

Steven's love for these beautiful "used up" thoroughbreds led him to consider the fate of the horses not so lucky to live at the Sanctuary. Some owners, particularly in small, less profitable horse tracks with smaller purses, simply discarded these beautiful animals when they could no longer make money. Without love for the animal, the cost of stabling, feeding and veterinarian services became a business decision. Arthritic thoroughbreds were often sold to horse slaughterers for as little as $200.

Even worse, Steven learned that many of these same animals were sold at horse auctions for consumption. Illegal in the United States, the horses were often shipped to Mexico and other countries that did not ban such consumption. Steven burned with rage as he thought, *How could the same humans who got such pleasure from these horses sentence them to this end?*

Steven now actively sought to rescue these animals before they reached their sad destinations. Often on the road, he would call Owie, "We got room for ten more rescues?" Soon the pasture fences were expanded to accommodate the happy animals who now had a second chance at life.

Steven became a voice for these animals, chastising his sport for ignoring this black eye. He urged media members he once knew to publicize this immoral practice, and made many appearances in thoroughbred governing bodies throughout the country.

One day Juanita and Steven watched another truck unload five more pardoned animals. One defeated horse, knots on a wild mane and tangled tail flying in all directions, limped out of the truck. The long white whiskers, similar to that of an old man, matched the color of the unkempt coat. Steven soon recognized his old friend, Majestic Max.

"Max, Max, it's me, Steven."

Max's dead ears rooted to the sky. Clumps of mud fell on Steven's arms as large nostrils inhaled a familiar scent. Juanita watched as a jubilant Steven grabbed the horse's neck.

"You're safe now Max. I'm going to take care of you."

Max's neglected coat took days of patient combing to untangle all the mats and grime. Medicine helped relieve the arthritis that made each step Max took so painful. But soon Max playfully awaited the carrots from his old friend each morning. Steven spoke affectionately to the horse, "You look like your old self Max."

Steven later learned Max's familiar racing tale from star to nobody. At five years of age Max tore a tendon in his right leg after another profitable campaign for David Moriarty. Max's new trainer rushed Max back into action, where he then tore the pastern bone in his left leg. Another six months of rehabilitation and Max was a different animal when he returned to action. Claimed from Moriarty's stable in a $20,000 claiming race, he was no longer an elite athlete. A crescendo of lower and lower claiming races found Max running in a small Texas track for a $3,000 purse. His fourth owner in two years sold him for $300 to a slaughterhouse. Fortunately, the Sanctuary saved this incredible white beauty from an inglorious death sentence.

Many days Steven would now saddle his old friend Max and wander the desert. If they were lucky, a herd of wild Mustangs, a billow of dust heralding their arrival, would gleefully cascade by them. Steven felt a surge of momentum in Max's body as he watched these resilient beasts roam the desert.

"Easy boy. Your roaming days are over."

While heading back to the stable after one such trip, Steven saw that the big house was adorned with blue balloons. A confused Steven considered, "Did I miss someone's birthday?"

Only Juanita came out and stood on the veranda to welcome them. She had a strange smile on her face.

"Everything okay, Juanita? What's with the balloons?"

"The blue is symbolic of a son, Steven. We are having a baby boy!"

Jumping off Max with a wild leap, he ran up and grabbed Juanita by the arms. "What, when? Are you sure?" he sputtered.

"I went to the doctor today. Owie drove me to Chelsea. I wanted to make sure before I told you. Are you happy?"

"Happy? I'm ecstatic," Steven yelled as he twirled Juanita in his arms.

Their marriage took place a month later on the veranda of the big house where the lovers once bared their painful pasts. Now their co-workers and staff tossed confetti on the couple who seemed focused on their promising future.

The couple's "honeymoon" was spent in a tent on a fertile bend of the Snake River, as undulating grass whispered them to sleep. Holding Junita close, Steven cried, "I wonder how my Sophia is doing." He hadn't seen her for seven years.

Since his last memory of her was in Court when she was six, he figured she was now thirteen. He wondered what the new teenager looked like. What her interests were. In his trips throughout the country he had asked colleagues whether anyone knew of Alyssa and Nicky Bianco's whereabouts. No one seemed to know anything, except that Nicky was not riding in any of the major racetracks. But most importantly, no one knew where their daughter now resided.

Juanita caressed Steven's head as he rested on her protruding belly.

"Sophia will be part of your life again, Steven. I'm sure of it. She will be a good sister to Steven Jr."

Steven had to be convinced to name his son after himself. "I haven't had the best of luck with the name, Juanita."

Juanita stubbornly held fast, "That was the old Steven. We have each other now."

As Juanita slept contently in the tent that night, Steven continued to cry. He cried, not for Sophia, but for the father he had never known, because he now knew the truth. For to his surprise his Mom had attended his Wyoming wedding. Her husband did not, being preoccupied with a softball tournament. But his mother had ventured out to the Wyoming desert.

As the wedding festivities came to an end, Carole had settled down on the veranda with Steven. As she gazed out at the animals roaming free in the fertile plains she spoke to her son, "I'm so proud of the man you have become. And Juanita is the perfect partner for you. I love her."

A contented Steven hugged his Mom. And then he urged her to tell him the secret about his dad.

Surprised, she finally said, "On one condition Steven, that it ends right here. You will not pursue the issue any further or seek any retaliation."

So, blind to what he was agreeing to, Steven consented to her conditions. And then she explained how his father had really died.

Chapter 20: Happy Life

STEVEN, NOW THIRTY, often had to pinch himself during the next four years of his contented life. His son Steven Jr. was born in a hospital ninety miles from the Snake River – the closest to the Sanctuary. Dark, thick hair covered the baby's head, his sun kissed complexion all Juanita. Blessed with the opportunity to be a father again, Steven relished his second chance. As soon as little Steven could walk, he roamed the stables with his dad. The staff at the Sanctuary came to assume Steven would be followed by the cheerful toddler. Junior would tug on Max's whiskers, while Max swatted a large tongue on the toddler in response.

Steven Jr. came to believe that everyone had a life like him. By four years old, the happy boy had his own pony, which he rode like an old cowboy in the paddock area. Everyone -including staff, volunteers, and visitors to the Sanctuary – was called "Auntie and Uncle" by the happy youngster with dark curls and chocolate eyes that melted everyone's heart. Many times Juanita had to warn her carefree son that people must do their work, and could not play with him all the time. But her heart filled with love and pride for her beautiful son and the wonderful place where her little family lived.

Steven tried to keep his trips outside the Sanctuary to a minimum. But word had gotten out that Wilson's Sanctuary was the place where thoroughbreds could be saved, and more and more horses were sent there. In fact Steven now paid death auctioneers not to slaughter the animals, but to hand them over to him. Fences were continually expanded in the vast paddocks that now held two hundred thoroughbreds. Stables, feeding, and bathing areas, and dormitories grew to accommodate the needs of horses and staff.

During one of his speaking events, Steven talked to Kentucky state legislators about banning the slaughter of thoroughbreds. Following a positive reception from those attending Steven was approached by an old friend, Jim Caldwell. No longer the hot-shot car dealership owner sporting tight jeans, Jim had liquidated all his car holdings. He was now a nationally known horse owner, who longed to win only the biggest of races like the Kentucky Derby and the Templeton Million. He dressed in the dark blue suit of a banker now, and cared about the image he portrayed.

After some small talk Jim got to his point, "Steven, ever think of getting back into horse training? I have lots of young yearlings coming up. Paid $950,000 today for one – a great grandson of Alex the Great."

That name brought memories to Steven of the epic race with Rumi Rose. "Not really Jim. I'm very happy with my life in Wyoming. Pops brought me there, and I don't think I can ever leave it."

Jim paused, "I understand Steven, but I can pay you a lot of money to train my stable. And Steven, don't worry about that ugly thing that happened years ago. No one believes you were ever guilty of that. I can get you a trainer's license tomorrow."

Without hesitation Steven answered, "Thank you Mr. Caldwell. I appreciate the offer. But I have a new wife and son, and I don't like leaving my family and home even for a day."

"Okay, but if you ever change your mind…"

As Jim Caldwell turned to leave, Steven recalled that Nicky Bianco was a jockey for Caldwell Stables. "Wait, do you know anything about Nicky Bianco or my ex-wife Alyssa?"

"I don't know where Nicky is. He hasn't ridden for me in three years. I heard he went bad using drugs and became unreliable as a jockey. Not sure if he's even riding anywhere these days. Alyssa seems to have disappeared."

"Thank you," said a disappointed Steven.

Unfortunately, the Sanctuary soon became a victim of its own success. Truck after truck unloaded old thoroughbreds from all over the country. All had been slated for slaughter, but escaped potentially ending up in the bellies of ignorant people.

One night Steven returned from another speaking engagement to find Juanita rustling papers on the dining room table. After returning from the kitchen with a cup of coffee, he gave a serious-looking Juanita a kiss. She removed her glasses and gave a sigh of concern.

"This is unsustainable Steven. We have gotten too big. We now have two hundred horses, and more coming in each month. Our vet bill alone was $20,000 last month, and that's with him giving us a break. Our grain fee is now $8,400 a month and rising. We need to expand the stable, and that will cost us $25,000 just for lumber. Owie said we have to hire two more staff just to care adequately for the animals. We make some money with tours, adoptions, and riding lessons, but more is owed than is coming in."

Juanita put her glasses down and quietly continued, "We might just have to stop taking in recues – at least for a while. Maybe we can get some other Sanctuary to help us."

Steven countered, "I have reached out to many of them. They have the same problem. There are just too many thoroughbreds being thrown away."

Raising his voice in agitation Steven vowed, "I'm not going to let these beautiful beasts be slaughtered. Never!"

Silence enveloped the couple in one of their rare disagreements of their four-year relationship.

Steven lay awake in bed that night, Juanita's breathing the only thing interrupting his busy mind. *Maybe we can get some government money to help us with the rescues,* he thought. But then he immediately dismissed this idea given his experience with politicians who had other priorities that would keep them reelected. The legislators had sensitively listened to Steven's speeches about giving racehorses care for all the enjoyment they had given to the public. But most states failed to pass any legislation banning the slaughter of these animals.

Steven remembered Pops's old words about horses, "They all fear people, and they have the right to fear them."

But Steven also knew that once these gorgeous animals trusted you, they would do anything for you. They would even die for people, as Steven well knew. "We domesticated these animals, and now they depend on us."

Tossing and turning next to Juanita, Steven remembered the offer from Jim Caldwell. *I wonder how much he might be willing to pay me.* A small part of Steven cherished the days when he trained his horses and man and animal achieved a common goal. Even his thoroughbreds knew when they had performed well and fulfilled their athletic prowess for which they had been created.

The "should nots" soon entered Steven's bedded mind. I will be away from my son, my wife, and this beautiful place. If I do train full time it will take 100% of my time, and I'm not even sure I'm still capable. On the other hand if I did become nationally known, I could be the thoroughbred activist that the sport needs. I would be in the national news, and people would take me more seriously than they would a former horse trainer.

The next morning Steven sat with his four year old son on his lap. Steven Jr. asked, "Daddy can we ride Max today?" Looking first at his son, and then at his wife sipping coffee, he addressed his tortured ambivalence, "I don't know Juanita. It would save the farm if I am successful, and I would have a national stage to prohibit horse slaughter. On the other hand I would be away from you and Steven Jr., and you would have to do all the heavy lifting here."

To his surprise Juanita voted for Steven to return to horse training. "Sometimes when we are on the veranda and you talk about the magic in training an animal to do what he loves to do, to run hard…you get a glint in your eye unlike any other time…except when little Steven asks you to ride Max. You have a special gift with horses Steven, and maybe these thoroughbreds need you to help them win."

Then Juanita put her arms around Steven's neck and whispered, "We will be fine here. In fact with you gone we will probably get less rescues." Eyeing little Steven who was still pulling on his father's hand to ride Max, she added, "Now go, take your son out to the desert."

And so, with Juanita's approval, Steven decided to call Jim Caldwell.

Chapter 21: Jim Caldwell's Stable

To SAY THAT JIM CALDWELL was all in as a nationally known horse owner was an understatement. He had created a syndicate with other businessmen that bred, bought and sold thoroughbreds. As importantly, his group were seen high fiving one another at major racetracks throughout the country. They loved the action of horseracing and being the envied faces of the sport. They flew in a private jet that displayed a large "C" on the exterior to races all over the world. To this group of partners who had made more money than they could ever spend, these junkets were exhilarations – something more to give them a high. And boy did they celebrate! Interviewers in the winner's circle had to withstand rich hijinks as owners poured beer on one another's heads.

But for all their success, one race had eluded them. For the last six years they had failed to win the Templeton Million. The race was now a misnomer – the race presently paid five million for the winning horse.

As Jim ushered Steven around his stables, he realized that's why Jim had hired him. "Every year we go up there to Kentucky, and get our asses kicked Steven. It's a long ride home for my boys who are used to celebrating in the winner's circle."

After walking around with Caldwell, Steven felt the name "stables" did not due justice to this operation. Air-conditioned horse stalls seemed fit for a Ritz Carlton guest. Horse bedding of the softest straw Steven had ever felt lined spotless stabler facilities. "We import the straw from all over the country," boasted Mr. Caldwell. Steven had to admit that he had no excuses if he did not succeed with Caldwell farms.

No need for human hot walkers in Caldwell's operation. Ten horses could be attached to octopus arms that walked horses at various speeds. An Olympic size pool filtered for horses' fetlocks offered a form of horse water therapy.

"Our horses have less injuries than horses in any other stable, Steven. Our veterinarians designed this pool just for equines."

Steven was tantalized by bathing and grooming of horses that resembled some high end spa.

"As you can see, Steven, we spare no expense. We want to win, and that's why we brought you here. I told my partners you somehow got more out of these animals than anyone I know."

Steven blushed, "I had a great teacher."

Caldwell responded, "Ah, Pops. What a nut. I heard he ended up living with the animals. Crazy guy."

Steven was silent. They would never understand Pops.

As Jim had predicted, Steven's renewed racehorse trainer's license was a quick formality. He could now train in any track in the country. Jim and his cigar smoking partners speedily agreed to

Steven's request of a $250,000 yearly salary, and 10% of the horses' winnings.

One of the overweight owners sputtered, "Money is secondary to us kid. We want the win. We figure we will start you at Falstaff Track in northern California. We got a bunch of two-year-olds up there that show lots of promise. That will get your feet wet. The Templeton Million is a year away. We got lots of other trainers on the payroll Steven, but we hope you're the one that takes us to the big prize."

After a quick visit to Wilson's Sanctuary to see his family, Steven went right to work at Falstaff. Steven met one of Caldwell's other trainers, Gerry Murphy. He eyed Steven warily. Each trainer was given five two-year-olds, as well as other horses to train. Both trainers knew that in this result orientated business, their success was based on horse wins.

As usual Steven spent most of his time understanding the personalities of these young horses. One in particular, a great grandson of Magnificent Max, and a half-brother of Majestic Max intrigued him. His name was Saucy Sully, and his fractions on workouts were superb – 46 seconds for four furlongs. But as a gifted athlete who sometimes takes his abilities for granted some days, Sully would often refuse to leave his stall. He preferred to munch the delicious barley Caldwell had imported from Ireland.

Steven's response: He had an older gelding named Mr. Pete, a pro's pro who gave his all even on workouts, humiliate Sully. On days Sully refused to pick up his legs on the track, Steve would have Pete go eyeball to eyeball with his lazy stablemate, then roar off leaving dust in Sully's face. After three such humiliations Saucy Sully got angry.

"Good boy," Steven whispered in Sully's ear back at the stable after the horse tore up a workout. "You know you are the best."

Sully's ears perked up as man and horse hot walked the old way, Steven talking to his equine friend as they went round and round the backside.

When Saucy Sully won his first race, pulling away by four lengths without a sweat Jim Caldwell could not be happier.

Saucy Sully's initial victory was followed by a party at the local country club. A proud Jim Caldwell approached Steven, "Why don't you come Steven. Celebrate with my partners and me."

"Thanks Mr. Caldwell, but I got another race tomorrow with your filly Jasmine. I think she could win."

"Really? She hasn't won in three months. She's going off at 20 to 1."

Steven smiled, "I think I got her figured out."

"About tonight Steven. Just make an appearance. It's good for business to be seen."

"Ok boss," said a resigned Steven.

Steven heard the boisterous male voices as he was ushered into a private boardroom at the country club. A group of about twelve bourbon hoisting men traded jokes and insults with each other. On two of their laps sat tight skirted women, their lean legs reminding him of his fillies. They laughed at crude jokes while brushing cigar smoke from their faces. The heavily made-up ladies looked young enough to be the men's daughters.

When they realized Steven was standing in their midst, the group cheered. "Nice win today." "You made us some money." Jim had a strange smile on his face as he handed Steven a bourbon.

"Drink, eat my friend. We got some entertainment tonight, if you know what I mean."

Steven made some necessary small talk with this group of bosses. After awhile they ignored the new trainer, and poured their attention on the young ladies. This gave Steven his opportunity to leave.

"Guys, got to go. Jasmine's running in the first race."

The fellow with the big belly ignored the lady on his lap to brag, "Jim told me Jasmine is live. I'm putting $10,000 on her. A bonus for you Steven if she wins."

Steven barely heard him as he raced out of the uncomfortable setting.

The next day, after Jasmine's second place finish a disappointed Steven talked with her jockey.

The disheartened jockey commented, "She would have won boss if the number one horse hadn't pinned me on the rail. She'll win the next time out."

A jubilant Jim came up and shook Steven's hand, "I bet her to win and place Steven. I just made $5,000 on her." Mr. Caldwell walked away with a huge smile on his face.

As Steven stood there, a young backsider placed a halter around Jasmine's head.

"Congratulations, Mr. Ricci," said the young feminine voice. "I met you last night at the party."

An incredulous Steven followed her as she began leading Jasmine back to her stall. "You were one of the girls at the party last night?'

"Yes, my name is Beth Allen."

"You looked so different last night. How old are you?"

"Nineteen," said the girl rather defensively.

"And you work on the backside?"

"Yeah. I work at different tracks for Mr. Caldwell."

As she disappeared down the track with Jasmine, Steven promised himself he would learn more about this young girl. But for now, he had two races tomorrow he was worried about.

The next morning Steven was working with another two-year-old thoroughbred he liked, Ms. Lulu. She was a filly with meticulous breeding. Her dappled chestnut coat was accentuated by a star shaped white marking on her forehead. All you had to know about Ms. Lulu was that the farrier refused to get near the animal. Ms. Lulu broke his hand when she objected to one of the nails going into her hoof. But Steven liked her fiery spirit. She reminded him of the leader of the wild Mustang pack in Wyoming, whose dominant nature kept them out of danger. "I'll figure this gal out," thought a confident Steven.

As Steven watched the new farrier gently replace Ms. Lulu's horseshoes, Jim Caldwell tapped him on the shoulder. "Cost me $350,000 for her Steven. What do you think?"

"I like her personality."

"Personality, shit. I bought her because she can run faster than any other horse."

"I know," said Steven, chewing on the soft hay, "But you can't measure a horse's heart. The horse has to want to win."

Jim seemed puzzled. "I guess," was the only response.

"By the way Jim, I saw that girl who was at the party the other night. Beth Allen. Does she work on the backside here?"

"Yeah, pretty girl huh."

"Is she around?"

"No, I had to send her to Kentucky this morning with some other workers. Why do you ask?"

"Ah, nothing really. But she looked so different the other night."

"Yeah, pretty girl. She should be back next month."

And with that Steven had to put Beth Allen out of his mind to concentrate on his demanding schedule. In the next six months Steven flew to races all over the country in Caldwell's private jet. Both Saucy Sully and Ms. Lulu were successful as the two year old campaign waged on. Sully won two of his first three races, while Ms. Lulu won a stakes victory. In all Steven was winning 40% of all his races, and soon acquired trainer Murphy's horses.

Once a month Steven returned to Wyoming to visit his family. Steven Jr.'s tears when he left made Steven want to quit. But Juanita encouraged him,

"The Farm is more solvent, and you are around the horses doing what you love."

As the calendar year progressed, and both Saucy Sully and Ms. Lulu turned three, Jim Caldwell turned giddy. "They have a new race at Templeton this year, the Temptress. We think Lulu and Sully can win both big races.

Steven tried to dampen his confidence, "They are both only three, going against some of the best older horses in the country Jim."

"Come on Steven. We have confidence in you. You'll get a bonus of a million if you win both Templeton races."

Not that he needed more motivation, Steven thought of what that kind of money could do for his horse Sanctuary.

With three months to go Caldwell moved his whole operation to Templeton Racetrack to prepare for the big races. Steven fought to control his emotions reliving all the good and bad memories from the stables of Kentucky. The first thing he did was to call his buddy Sal to visit him. "And don't bring any cigarettes to the backside. No smoking around my horses." Soon a proud Sal was playing gin rummy card games on the backside, and taking hard earned money from the groomers.

One of those groomers was the young woman Beth Allen, whom Steven had not seen since Falstaff. "You didn't get back to California, I see, Beth."

"No," said the girl, dressed in faded jeans, and a worn blue tee shirt.

"How have you been?"

“Without makeup, the angel-faced girl looked so young. As she blew back the straight blonde hair that had fallen into her face, she said, “Mr. Caldwell has me working all over the place. But I’ll be here until the big Templeton races are over.”

“Great,” said Steven. “Looking forward to working with you. Let me know if you need anything.” Then Steven hurried off to his myriad of assignments.

Chapter 22: The Templeton Million

AS THE TEMPLETON LOOMED within the next month Steven was practically living in the stables. One of his frequent visitors was Beth Allen. Steven came to believe that Beth hid behind that stringy blonde hair that covered her eyes. He remembered how differently she had acted the night he saw her at the owners' party.

Steven and Beth shared one thing, a love for thoroughbreds. Beth loved to bathe and then polish the coats of all the horses, but particularly Ms. Lulu.

"I wish I could be like her," said a wistful Beth one day as she brushed conditioner in Lulu's chocolate coat. "She's so confident. It's like she knows she will win the Temptress.

"She has the confidence of the Mustangs in the Wyoming desert Beth. No one can tell them what to do. You will have to come out to my Sanctuary some day Beth. You will love it."

"Yes, I would love that. But me and the girls don't have a lot of free time."

"The girls?" Steven asked.

"Ah, nothing, Mr. Ricci. Your farm sounds wonderful."

Each day Steven would arrive at the stables at 4 a.m. to find Beth already cleaning the stalls of Saucy Sully and Ms. Lulu.

"No more brushing them today, Beth," Steven laughed. "You're going to polish their coats off before the big race."

During their conversations, Steven and Beth revealed more and more about themselves. Steven showed Beth pictures of his wife and son.

"Your wife is so beautiful. I wish I had skin like her, so exotic. I look like an Iowa hick with my cornstalk skin."

Steven smiled, "You look fine, particularly without all that makeup."

One day as the two were working, Beth talked about herself. "I had the best childhood in Iowa, Mr. Ricci. We lived on a farm that my dad's family has owned for three generations. I fed chickens, milked cows, and even won a 4H prize for my goat Daisy. But my mom wasn't cut out for that life. She was a California girl who met my dad when he was stationed in San Diego." Then she added sarcastically, "He sweet talked her about the great farm life. I get it, her first love at nineteen. My dad, handsome in his uniform sweeping her off her feet."

"The reality was she came to hate the farm life. When I was seven, she went to her high school reunion, and met her old boyfriend. It was a crazy divorce, and I ended up with her in San Diego."

"Did your mom marry the boyfriend?"

"Yeah, it lasted all of six months."

As she prepared Saucy Sully's food bin Beth adopted the cynical tone of a parent who had been let down by two adolescents. "It's funny. After the divorce my dad had me out to the farm, but he was different. He seemed to have no interest in me except to hit me with questions about who my mother was dating. Mr. Ricci, I got tired of it, and didn't want to go out there anymore."

"How about your mom, Beth?"

"Well, it was just me and her, and she was making up for lost time with her single life. It was like I was in the way. Sometimes I went to my grandparents for a while, and then I'd go back to my mom's. We moved five times in two years."

"That must have been hard on you, Beth, all alone, constantly changing friends and schools."

"Yeah, my grades went down, and I just felt like I was all alone. That's how I got in with some friends who introduced me to Caldwell."

"Were you in high school?"

At that point Beth wiped the tee shirt over her eyes, and said, "I got to go Mr. Ricci."

A week before the Templeton Steven was doing facetime with Steven Jr. "Son, I'll be home next week. Can't wait to take you out on Max."

Beth watched the interaction.

"Want to say hi to my son Beth?"

Beth waved to the boy. "Hi Steven. I'm Beth."

After the phone call Steven and Beth went about preparing Lulu for her last workout before the Temptress.

"Your son is lucky Mr. Ricci. He has someone to look out for him."

"Yes. But I also have a daughter I've not seen in years, Beth. Things happened and we got estranged, but I hope to see her again. I don't even know how to reach her. So you now know I'm not perfect."

"Oh yes you are Mr. Ricci. If I had you for a dad I probably wouldn't be doing what I'm doing."

A concerned Steven would not evade the issue this time. "Beth, just what are you doing?"

Looking away Beth said, "Working here."

"No Beth. What's going on with these older men?"

"Okay Mr. Ricci, I'll tell you, but you got to keep it a secret. I don't want anyone to get in trouble. And for the first time I can buy anything I want. I could never afford my apartment if I didn't do it."

"Do what?" persisted Steven.

"You know, entertain the guys. Keep them happy."

"Are you talking about having sex with those old guys?"

"Please, Mr. Ricci…I can't say anything else."

"But the new Steven, the one who was falsely accused of a sex crime and came out a better man, would not let it go. "Please Beth, tell me what's going on. How did this happen?"

"Well I told you my mom was doing her own thing when I was in high school. I was hanging out with some kids and smoking pot. I didn't care much about school. My friend Tracy knew this older girl who said we could make lots of money being around these older men and going on trips with them."

"So you were only sixteen years old when they recruited you?"

"I was seventeen, and an adult. No one else was watching out for me!"

"How many of these girls are there?"

"Six or seven, but most of them are 18."

"Most?"

"Well, some of the guys like real young girls. They call them cheerleaders. We sometimes get girls from high school to come to our parties. Look, it's not all that bad. We laugh at these guys because they think we really care about them. They take us in their private jet to meet their friends in the racing business. It's not hard work. I just zone out."

"When you're having sex with older guys?"

Beth continued, a defensive tone in her voice, "All I know is that I can buy anything I want. All the girls are going to Cabo after the Templeton." Then she smiled, "We will need a vacation after all the parties."

Steven saw no humor in the poor joke. "Look Beth, this is not right. It might look good now, but you're going to regret these decisions. These men are going to want more and more. Don't you see that these old men are trafficking you! I've got to do something to stop it."

Beth stormed out of Ms. Lulu's stall in tears. "I knew I shouldn't have told you. You're just like my mom, trying to wreck my life."

Steven called in vain for Beth to come back, as Ms. Lulu's eyes widened in anxiety. "Calm down girl," Steven said as he contemplated this grave situation.

Later that night a distraught Steven called Juanita. “I don’t know what to do. Should I tell Caldwell what I know?”

Juanita commiserated, “Look, a man capable of using these girls is not going listen to you.

“I know, I know, but the race is only three days away.”

“Maybe you should wait until after the race to address this.”

“No…no. If I win Beth said the girls will work at all the celebrating sex parties.”

Juanita then said something she regretted the rest of her life, “At least if we wait the Sanctuary will get some of the winnings.”

“But how can I live with myself? I don’t know what to do.”

After a sleepless night, Steven had thoughts of Sophia. “She would be about 18 now. That could be her being used by these perverts.”

Steven dressed quickly in the morning. He had made his decision. He would go to the police.

Chapter 23: Racing Treachery

THE NEXT MORNING AT 5 A.M. Steven was hard at work massaging Saucy Sully's legs. The trainer's fingers worked the fetlock tendons near the horse's ankles that are so important for flexion. "Good boy Sully," Steven murmured. "In two days, the whole country will know about you." As if agreeing, Sully snorted and shook his head affirmatively.

He was interrupted by his boss Jim Caldwell. "Well, Steven, what do you think? Is he ready?"

Hands carefully kneading Sully's ankles, Steven reassured the owner, "Ready as he will ever be."

Probing a bit further Jim said, "and Lulu?"

"I think we have a great chance to win both."

"Just the confidence I like to hear. Look, you've got to come to the victory parties after the races. My partners insist on it."

"Probably, boss, but after that I'm going back to Wyoming for about a month."

Jim smiled and said, "Sure, just win the races first."

With that the jaunty owner started to exit the barn, then turned back and asked, "Everything else okay with you, Steven?"

"Sure, why?"

"Oh, nothing."

When he finished his morning work Steven called the Chief of Police.

Later that day Steven walked into the Arcadia police station. Chief David Powell invited Steven into his office, which was adorned with citations from all over the state of Kentucky.

Chief Powell shushed Steven as he attempted to introduce himself, “I know who you are. In two days you’re going to be the most famous person in Kentucky.” Powell laughed, “Shit, win the Templeton and Temptress, and you’ll be on the cover of Time Magazine!”

Steven was in no mood to talk about racing today. “Chief Powell, I have become aware of a terrible situation. Horse owners are using girls, some underage, for sex. I’ve talked to one of these girls who worked for me. She was underage when she started, and she was recruited by other girls. I think it’s a big operation. They are flying these young girls all over the country for this stuff.”

Chief Powell leaned back in his chair, seemingly in deep thought. “This is a very serious accusation Mr. Ricci. If what you say is true, these men are guilty of trafficking underage girls throughout the country. That is a federal charge and will involve the F.B.I. and the Department of Justice. Are you committed to taking these charges all the way? You might have to wear a wire to get proof of this.”

“I’ll do whatever it takes to stop this operation. I have a daughter their age Chief. It’s not right.”

“So, even if it affects your ability to train horses, you’re all in?”

"Chief, I love horses. But this is about violation of young human life. I'll do anything to stop it."

"All right then, I'll contact the District Attorney's office. Just realize this won't be resolved soon. It might take months of investigation to get an indictment against these men. Until then, don't say anything else until you hear from me."

"Okay Chief, but what should I do in the meantime?"

"Just take notes of any other information, and any other people who can substantiate what you say. And one more thing, just win the races on Saturday."

Steven remembered these words long after. He was puzzled by the levity of the Chief's remark at such a serious time.

On Thursday evening at 10 p.m. some thirty-six hours before the Templeton, Steven was alone in Saucy Sully's stall watching him contently munch on his expensive oats. "Good boy," Steven said admiringly, as Sully could not look better in his trainer's eyes. Steven knew one thing, he might work for another owner after the Templeton, but he was all done with Caldwell Stable. He would see through the legal proceedings, but he was done with Jim Caldwell and his cronies.

Deep in thought, Steven was startled by Beth Allen, who seemed to appear out of nowhere. "Beth, I'm so happy to see you. I know you were upset with me the other day."

Glassy eyed Beth seemed different. She was unaware of her surroundings, her angry eyes focused on Steven. "You shouldn't have said anything Mr. Ricci." With that Beth jumped on Steven, aggressively punching and kicking him. He felt her teeth tear at his skin as he battled back defensively. Her strength surprised Steven as he tried unsuccessfully to pin her arms behind her. She tore at his skin scratching his face like a mindless zombie. Then she started shouting, "Leave me alone, you pervert! Help! Help!" She shouted again and again, as she now scratched herself.

Backstretch security, hired to protect thoroughbreds worth millions came running in with their flashlights. "Mr. Ricci, are you okay?" said the agents familiar with the famous trainer.

Before he could respond, Beth screamed, "Why you asking him? He tried to rape me!"

Dazed, Steven looked at the young girl with torn clothing, and raw self-inflicted wounds on her face and neck. "Beth, what are you doing?" he asked breathlessly, tired after going toe to toe with this ferocious girl. Steven turned to the guards, "You've got to believe me. She attacked me. I know she was put up to it."

The confused security guards, a good gig for local guys making $20 per hour to watch sleeping horses, did the only thing they could do. They called the police.

The rest of the night became a hangover blur. Beth was taken to the local hospital, treated for her injuries, and tested for rape. Steven was handcuffed, photographed, and placed in a cell. He was remanded there over the weekend, until a probable cause hearing, scheduled for him for the following Monday. Steven was allowed a phone call that Friday morning. He called Juanita in Wyoming. At first she could not even make out his garbled words in between tears. Eventually she understood his words and understood what had happened.

"You were set up Steven. I'll catch the first flight there."

Steven's next call was to his former attorney, Morris Stuart. The lawyer-client relationship had long passed, and the two were friends. In fact, Attorney Stuart had visited the Sanctuary last year when he was in Wyoming for business. He had been so happy at the positive changes in Steven, recognizing immediately that the former trainer was at peace with his new life. Stuart vowed to Juanita Saturday morning before going to the jail that he would do everything in his power "to right this terrible wrong." He knew Steven was not capable of such a terrible act. But he was also aware that he was dealing with powerful people who would do anything to keep themselves out of jail.

Attorney Stuart was concerned when he saw Steven slumped in his chair in the dirty conference room in the county jail. He thought Steven had the defeated look of a man guilty of something.

Steven looked hopelessly at his attorney and said, "I should be getting my horses ready for the races today, Morris. Instead I'm back where you first met me." Putting his hands over his face in shame he continued, "I can't believe she could do this to me."

Attorney Stuart spoke firmly as he addressed his client and friend, "Steven take your hands away from your face. Look, you are not guilty of anything. Now act like it! This girl didn't have a chance with these monsters. They probably both threatened and enticed her and may have drugged her on top of that. Every adult in her life has probably used her, so she is operating on survival instinct."

" You're right Morris. I just… I was so surprised and troubled by what she said and did. She's a nice girl, but she's young and vulnerable. She reminded me of my daughter who I wish I had in my life."

Steven told his attorney about his visit to Police Chief Powell. "You've got to talk to him. I warned him about the sex trafficking. That gives these men reason to want to frame me."

Attorney Stuart drew on his legal experiences with the rich and powerful. "Steven, I bet there is no record of your visit to the Chief. I hope I'm wrong, but he's probably already on the owners' payroll. This charge of rape is no coincidence to your bringing up allegations against these powerful men. Chief Powell probably knew about what was happening with these girls and the owners."

As if not depressed enough already, Steven moaned," I just want to go back to Wyoming. I told Juanita I was done with Caldwell after today anyway. Do you think I can go to jail again for something I did not do?"

Attorney Stuart tried to be optimistic to his innocent friend, but he also had to be realistic. "Your arraignment is on Monday Steven, to be followed by a probable cause hearing in about a month. I'm going to try to get you out on bail Monday, but the wrongful felony with your daughter might affect this. A friendly Judge may allow your past incarceration to be revealed to the jury."

Steven countered, "And how long will it be until the trial?"

"Could be up to a year Steven. These things unfortunately move slowly in the legal arena."

A defeated Steven was then led back to the tiny cell he shared with an alcohol reeking man charged with driving under the influence. Later that Saturday afternoon Steven called the guards because his semiconscious cellmate had defecated on himself. As the guards led the still inebriated man to the showers, one guard called back to Steven, "By the way both your horses lost today."

The next day Steven found himself sharing palms with Juanita, the couple's loving hands separated by two inches of glass. They talked by phones that had not been cleaned in months. Juanita's regal features were replaced by drooping eyelids and watery eyes. With a trembling voice she asked her husband, "What does your attorney say? When can you get out of here?"

"Hopefully tomorrow, but my old case might work against me." Please Juanita, you have to stay strong. Steven Jr. needs you. God will provide for us. He knows I am innocent."

Juanita gave him a brief smile, and showed him the rosary clutched tightly in her hands. "I never spent so much time on my knees praying for God to help us," she said.

Steven knew he had to show strength for his family. "I've been knocked down before Juanita. I can handle it."

"What did you learn about the Templeton and Temptress yesterday?" he asked Juanita.

"From what I read, Ms. Lulu threw her jockey as the gate opened. She was riderless, but won the race by ten lengths."

Steven smiled even though he knew she was disqualified. "She knew something was not right. She was just pissed."

"How about Saucy Sully?"

"He had an early lead in the Templeton, but got tired and lost by eight lengths."

Steven thought, "He lost his confidence without me. I know that." Steven recognized that both horses had an important relationship with him.

Steven commented, "I guess the media is all over the place with this story."

Juanita grimaced, "I had to fight through them to get in here. They were shouting all kinds of nasty questions at me. I heard that Jim Caldwell held a press conference in front of Sully's stall Friday to say that he was "surprised" and "disappointed" by your arrest. He added that he had full confidence your co-trainer Gerry Murray could win both races.

On Monday morning Steven shuffled into Court in the same clothes he was wearing when he was arrested. The prosecutor's office showed photos of a bruised and swollen faced young victim who was allegedly attacked in a horse's stall by the defendant.

He then stated, "In addition, the defendant was incarcerated for sexual molestation of his own daughter and served time in state prison for this crime."

Attorney Stuart, the defending attorney protested vigorously that the previous charges were dismissed by the Appeals Court, but to no avail. Steven's senses were numb, and he barely heard the Judge deny bail, labeling this defendant "a potential sexual predator".

Assisted to his feet by two beefy court officers, Steven mouthed to his distraught wife, "Go home to the Sanctuary."

For the next several months Steven reacquainted himself to the detachment of humanity that is prison life. Except for brief legal procedural hearings, Steven's lethargy was only lessoned by phone talks with Juanita and Steven Jr. When Juanita asked about coming to visit, Steven would answer, "No, I don't want you to come here. Take care of Steven Jr. and the Sanctuary. "That's all I want."

Steven cried after phone calls with his son. "Yes, daddy still loves you. I'll be home soon."

Their phone conversations always ended in the same way, with Steven's plea, "You take care of Mom, Son. She needs you now."

"Yes, daddy," responded Steven Jr., a seven year old boy trying to sound like a man.

The trial was scheduled for the following spring, nine long months away. Steven was not optimistic, even though he placed his faith in God each morning on his knees in prayer. Attorney

Stuart had subpoenaed all of Chief Powell's records, and deposed him. The Chief had no records of any interview with Steven Ricci about sex trafficking and would testify to that.

"I'm not surprised," said a grim faced Attorney Morris Stuart.

Adding to this pessimism was Attorney Stuart's failure to keep Steven's prior conviction involving his daughter out of the jury's consideration. "I'll appeal this ruling Steven, but for now the jury will hear of your past incarceration. As blow after legal blow reigned on Steven, the only thing that kept him sane were the daily phone calls with his wife and son.

The trial that took place that spring unfolded like a cruel joke. At one point a DNA expert detailed that Steven's skin was found under the victim's fingernails, and on her scratches. Steven scanned the jury and in his mind he perceived the look of guilty on their faces.

The prosecutor declared, "This guy is a danger who has a thing for young girls."

The highlight of the trial was the appearance of the victim Beth Allen. Appearing like a young college student in a neat gray dress, black sweater, and soft blonde curls, she confidently strode into Court. The only time she looked at Steven was when the prosecutor asked her to identify the source of her anguish. And her anguish was plausible, as she continually dabbed at her eyes during her testimony. She recounted how much she idolized the famous trainer who built such strong relationships with racehorses.

"We bonded on our love for horses," she stated.

She then relayed how Mr. Ricci had encouraged her to help him care for Ms. Lulu and Saucy Sully.

On the night of the alleged attempted rape Ms. Allen testified that she was surprised when Mr. Ricci invited her to the stable late at night. "He had never done that before." She alleged that he had a "funny" look on his face as he cornered her in a stall next to Ms. Lulu.

"He started putting his hands all over me, and I told him to stop. When he didn't I tried to escape, but he blocked the entrance. I knew I had to fight to get out of there."

Recounting the physical battle that quickly escalated, Ms. Allen continued, "I kept screaming and screaming for help." Tears now streamed down her face. "Thank God the guards came. That's the only thing that saved me."

The youthful Beth Allen withstood the strong cross examination by Attorney Stuart. Steven's attorney had predicted that her testimony would be rehearsed, but even Steven marveled at this Oscar performance. *None of it is true, but if I was on the jury I'd believe her,* Steven told himself.

Ms. Allen denied any sex trafficking or abuse by any owners. "They gave me a job around horses, when no one else would."

Attorney Stuart was also thwarted at every turn in obtaining evidence about other girls who were also involved in this sex conspiracy. They seemed to have disappeared overnight. They were untraceable with false identities, and no record of income. Steven had told Attorney Stuart, "Beth told me all the girls get paid in cash."

The jury reached a decision in less than six hours. As Steven rose to learn his fate, he realized that every Juror averted his gaze. He was found guilty on two charges: attempted rape and attempted sexual battery. He never heard the Judge's gruff voice pronounce sentence, nor impart admonishment that he was a "sexual danger to society."

No, Steven had turned to look at Juanita, who had fallen to her knees as the sentence was pronounced. He mouthed his love for her as he was taken away. Juanita's rosary was later picked up by a court officer. Ten years incarceration was the societal penalty for the guiltless Steven Ricci. The second time he had been wrongfully convicted. Would the innocent Steven survive a second stint in hell?

Chapter 24: A Second Imprisonment

STEVEN PREPARED FOR HIS SECOND sojourn in Lennox Penitentiary in northern Kentucky. "I'm not sure I can take ten years up there Morris."

"You will," said his attorney, "because you know you are innocent. I will begin the appeal process immediately. I'm very confident I can get you a new trial. The jury should never have heard about your first wrongful conviction."

As Attorney Morris spoke Juanita held firmly to Steven's hand, as if she would never let it go.

"Please Juanita, go back to the Sanctuary. Tell Steven Jr. I love him, and how proud I am of him. Take care of things. Owie has promised to help you run things without me."

Husband and wife had tears in their eyes as they hugged each other tightly. Their promises seemed meaningless at this point, but Juanita made Steven make one more promise. "Promise me you will come home Steven," she pleaded. And with a sad smile he said he would.

Two burly guards interrupted the trio. "Times up Ricci. Got to go to Lennox now." Steven inhaled Juanita's presence. He would long remember this last touch of his wife.

Head down, he bounced in a prison van for the next four hours, his journey ending at the familiar fortress.

Steven was a bit of a celebrity in prison, given the well-publicized events surrounding the Templeton horse race and his subsequent arrest. "I lost $100 bucks on Saucy Sully," shouted one of the inmates as Steven was led into his cell. But the notoriety of the case and Steven's great personal fall led even the inmates to give him some sympathy.

One of the older inmates, a mafia don who would never get out of Lennox, cornered Steven one day in the yard. "I think you got a raw deal. Those horses would have won with you there." He added ominously, "I told everyone, even the guards, not to fuck with you or they will answer to me." Then he smirked, "Eh, we got to take care of people whose last name ends in a vowel."

Steven thanked him, but also realized he did not want more of a relationship with this leader. "We have homemade pasta every Saturday night with fresh parmesan kid. You're welcome to join us." Politely, Steven refused.

Steven did get one break. His first job request was to work at the prison library. Perhaps due to the influence of the Mafia killer, Steven was made a trustee of the library. That gave him unlimited access to the considerable well-stocked library.

Naturally, Steven's interest turned to books about thoroughbreds. He learned that the breed was created in England in the late 17th and early 18th centuries. Three stallions imported from the Middle

East were mated to elite English mares. All modern thoroughbreds can be traced to one of these three horses: Byerley Turk, Darley Arabian, and Godolphin Arabian. Amazed, Steven thought, *Wow, in over three hundred years all thoroughbreds share the same ancestors. That's what makes them so special.*

Steven also learned that by 1809, England had established its own jockey club as well as a Triple Crown of three professional flat races. In the United States, thoroughbred racing prospered after the Civil War. Remarkably, the first Belmont stakes race was held in 1867.

Steven became engrossed in learning more about his beloved horses. He read biographies of legendary horses such as Man O' War, Seabiscuit, and Citation. Each day led him to another facet of the beautiful animals he admired so much. And it helped the time go by quicker. Every day he talked to Juanita and Steven Jr. "No," he told her when she asked to visit him, "Don't come here Juanita. Stay at the Sanctuary. I'm alright."

Steven patiently listened to Attorney Stuart tell him that his appeal was winding its way forward. But mentally Steven had given up on that. He was hoping that in five years he would be let out on good behavior.

So a year later he was surprised to learn that he had a visitor. His face reddened when he heard the name, Sophia Ricci. As Steven was led to the guest area, he mentally computed that his daughter would be about twenty years old. He was both excited and nervous. How would she react to the man who abandoned her? To the man she identified in Court as her abuser some fourteen years ago?

Steven met a Ricci face as palpable and anxious as his own.

“Hi Dad,” Sophia said without making eye contact.

“Hi Sophia,” he stammered, “I always missed you.”

Sophia’s head shot up, “How come you didn’t try to find me?”

Steven did not have the words to respond at first. He simply gazed at the young woman before him dressed in a red sweater, jeans and sneakers. He took in her sandy brown hair, sharp nose and dimpled chin. He marveled, “If I could walk out of here beside her everyone would know she is my daughter.”

The long silence ended with Steven awkwardly touching his daughter’s hands since his hands were handcuffed. “Can you remove these?” Steven asked the guard who was slumped in the corner watching this family reunion. The guard shook his head negatively.

Steven turned back to his daughter, “Honey I did write letters to you. I guess they never got to you. But part of me simply felt I didn’t deserve you. I was such a bad father to you and bad husband to your mother.”

“I thought about you a lot dad. I felt guilty with everything that happened.”

Steven winced, “I didn’t think our reunion would be in a prison honey.”

“I’m okay dad. I’m really happy to see you.”

Grabbing Sophia's hands Steven said, "And I'm so happy you came to see me. I think I'm a much better person than I was when I was younger. Sophia some good people have changed my life. I'd love you to be part of my new life." As Steven spoke to his daughter his eyes were riveted to her Irish blue eyes.

Sophia too looked deep into to her father's eyes as she responded, "I always loved you dad."

Emotions buried by years of separation seemed to melt quickly. Sharing memories left father and daughter comfortably laughing and crying over the next hour.

"Sophia, you are so beautiful," he said to his daughter as they sat next to each other, ignorant of the guard in their midst. "Tell me about your life." Confidently Sophia said she was about to become a sophomore at the University of California. Steven beamed.

"Dad, I think I might want to be a veterinarian. I'm a science major."

"Wonderful. You must come out to my horse sanctuary in Wyoming Sophia." In a breathless monologue Steven told his daughter about Juanita and her brother Steven Jr. "They would love to meet you, Sophia."

"Oh dad, I would love to," Sophia said, as Steven rattled on about the wild Mustangs that roam near his farm.

The smile in his eyes disappeared as Steven said, "I had a wonderful life Sophia until this thing happened. You know I didn't touch that girl."

"Yes, dad, I believe you. That's how I was able to find out about you. I saw those terrible reports in the news."

Their two hours together flew by when the slumbering officer in the corner awoke and shouted, "Time's up Ricci." A handcuffed Steven touched his daughter's hand. "My next allowed visit is in two days. Will you come back?"

"Sure dad."

As Steven was led back to his cell, random thoughts exploded in his mind. Neither had discussed the sexual abuse charges. Should he leave the topic in the gutter where it belonged?

Two days later Steven quickly walked to the visitation room. "Slow down Ricci," said his portly guard. Again his daughter greeted him with a warm hug he awkwardly tried to return with his handcuffed hands. He re-examined his daughter's handsome features, and bursting with pride he said, "Sophia, you turned out beautiful in every way." Sophia just blushed.

"Tell me about your mom. Is she okay?"

"Yes, she is remarried. She met a dentist in the small town of Calvert in northern California where we were living. Her name is now Alyssa Williams. He's a nice guy. She's happy. She deserves that."

Softly Steven said, "And Nicky Bianco?"

"We haven't seen him in four years. He took a fall at a racetrack a few years back. He started abusing pills and alcohol. First to keep the weight off when he returned to racing, but he became addicted." Sophia looked away, "He was very mean to Mom. He blamed you for all his problems, which led to blaming her when he got high." Then tearing up Sophia added, "He became violent to her. Finally she got a restraining order and kicked him out. He never even showed up for the divorce. No one knows where he is now."

"And Damien? Is he okay?"

"He lives with Mom and her husband, although Damien is not nice to him. He saw a lot of arguing and fighting between mom and Nicky. Damien was very close to his dad. He almost lived at the track with his father when he was young. He took the divorce hard. I'm really worried about him. He doesn't talk a lot. He's got lots of pent-up anger in him. But Mom keeps a close eye on him."

"I see," said Steven reminiscing that Sophia was also by his side in the backside when she was a child. Silence then enveloped the father and daughter, an uncomfortable silence.

"Dad," said Sophia finally breaking the silence, "I want you to know I'm sorry for the Court thing. I know it didn't happen."

"That's okay honey." As they held hands Steven asked, "Can I ask you one thing? Did Nicky put you up to it?"

Sophia pulled back immediately, "Mom told me you would take revenge on Nicky if I said anything."

"Honey, I'm different now. Yes, the old Steven might have done so. My life is with Juanita and your brother. You are part of that life now. I just need to know for my own mental state. You see, I felt like such a neglectful dad that I was guilty of something. I just want to know what happened."

"Promise me dad, that you will never seek revenge on Nicky."

"Yes, Sophia, I will never seek revenge on Nicky for these false charges."

Sophia then took a deep breath, "I've thought a lot about those days and I even got therapy, but things are still murky. I do remember Nicky would always say, "Make sure your dad does not touch you anywhere." Nicky was obsessed about that. You remember Mom was resting a lot, then when she was pregnant with Damien, Nicky would change me and ask lots of questions about how you put on my pajamas. He said it so much that after a while I got nervous about you changing me. Then all these other people started asking me if you touched me. I said yes just to end all the questions."

"I see Sophia. I loved your visits with me. You know I would never hurt you."

"I know dad. I remember those Saturday mornings watching cartoons with you and my stuffed horse Max."

The couple laughed, recalling those happy times spent together. After a while Sophia offered one more thing. "Nicky used to give me a bubble bath just before visits with you. He knew I loved to play with the bubbles. He poured something in the bath to make the bubbles. I only remember it since he did it only when Mom was asleep."

Steven suspected that whatever Nicky did caused Sophia's urinary infections. But he did not share these thoughts with his daughter.

Sophia's weekly visits continued through the month of August. During one of those visits she told her dad, “Dad, I’ll be going back to school in September. I’ll try to come as often as I can.”

“No, honey. You concentrate on school. I ‘ll be fine. When I get out of here I want you to meet your family in Wyoming. Here, take Juanita’s number. She would love to talk to you.”

The tenor of the father-daughter meetings changed in those four weeks. Sophia became obsessed with knowing the details of the sex trafficking case in Templeton. She wanted to know who was involved, and how did the false charge of rape occur. Steven attempted to divert the conversation to the charms of the Snake River, but to no avail. His daughter persisted in learning as much as Steven could tell her about the horse owners and victims of the sex trafficking.

And then August turned into September. Sophia had to leave the cheap hotel she had rented near the Lennox prison. Father and daughter gave each other a deep hug.

“I’m so proud of you Sophia. Some day when you are a vet you can take care of the horses at Wilson Sanctuary. I’d love that.”

The images of that moment became a distant memory for Steven in the next year and a half. Prison life erases the promises of a life that is free, replacing those promises with baring despair. Even reading about famous thoroughbreds had lost its appeal. Steven’s one joy was lying in bed and imagining the plains of Wyoming where the Mustangs ran wild.

The sad tempo of prison life was disrupted one day as Steven began his third year of incarceration.

A guard beat his night stick against a sleeping Steven's prison cell.

"Hey Ricci, I heard they arrested one of the horse owners who put you in prison."

A groggy Steven did not immediately realize that he had just hit a life trifecta.

Chapter 25: A Surprise

LATER THAT DAY, STEVEN WAS USHERED into the office of the Prison Superintendent. Steven couldn't believe such an attractive non-gray room even existed in Lenox. In the center of the room was a dark walnut desk facing three red captain's chairs. His eyes immediately went to the occupants of these three chairs: Juanita, Sophia, and his mom Carole. The desk and chairs sat on a plush charcoal rug. Sitting behind the desk in a stylish black leather chair was a smiling Morris Stuart, the first sign that this was to be an unusual day in Steven's life.

The second unusual aspect of the day was that the guard had not handcuffed Steven. "You'll find out why," said the smiling guard. He found out why when the overwhelmed Steven ran to hug the three women who buried him in kisses.

Tearing himself away from the joyous encounter Steven finally asked Morris, "What's up?"

"Well, because of your daughter Sophia we have a hearing later today to release you from here. Last week indictments were handed down against Jim Caldwell and seven other horse owners for conspiracy to sex traffic minors. In addition, all eight men were charged with conspiracy for interstate transport of adult women for prostitution. These are just the Federal charges Steven. Many states are fighting over jurisdiction to bring their own charges against these predators.

"How?" "What?" said a stunned Steven as he fell into one of the plush chairs.

Juanita interjected, "Steven, it's too complicated to digest now. All you need to know is your daughter, Sophia, went underground to infiltrate these people."

Steven grabbed his daughter's hand, "Are you okay? Did they do anything to you?"

A smiling Sophia reassured him, "I was too smart for those perverts Dad."

Several hours later, a still dazed Steven was led into Court. A surprised Steven heard the prosecutor's attorney say, "In light of the testimony of one Beth Allen who will be our primary informant of this conspiracy, we have no objection to the release of Steven Ricci. She has rescinded her rape claims against Mr. Ricci as she informed the Court she was coerced by the defendants to make false claims."

The Judge's stern gaze disheartened Steven, but his words did not. "In light of this information the Court determines exceptional evidence to allow Mr. Ricci temporary release pending the results of the trial. Mr. Ricci keep in mind that you will be on probation during this period, and subject to the Court's jurisdiction."

Steven raised his hand, "Your Honor, I have one request. Can I go home to Wyoming? You see I have a horse sanctuary and …"

The Judge quickly put up his hand, "I think we can arrange for probation officers to supervise you in Wyoming."

Juanita kissed Steven as he tried to thank the Judge. Smothered in kisses Steven could barely say, "Let's go home."

Flying above the panoramic prairies and mountains of Wyoming, Steven squeezed his wife's hand. "I've never been happier." Joining the happy couple were Sophia, and Steven's mother Carole.

Arriving at the Sanctuary, Sophia hoisted a smiling ten year old Steven into her arms. In contrast, the silky blonde hair against the dark curls did not conflict their affection for one another. "I'm so happy to meet you my little brother."

But soon Jr. was ensconced in Steven's arms. "I'll never leave you again Steven." In the distance the rescued thoroughbreds gathered in the corals, seemingly knowing that Steven had returned. The staff at the Sanctuary welcomed Steven home. "Thank you everyone. Come up to the big house to celebrate."

The party lasted until the early morning hours. As the house finally grew quiet Steven and his daughter ventured out to the veranda, the stars in the night sky sparkling like diamonds.

"Tell me what happened honey."

"Well, first I took a semester off from college. I knew this was going to take some time. I changed my name and got a new I.D. I was now Sophia Clark. I familiarized myself with the legal case. They are all public documents. And then I talked with lots of the workers on the backside. They wouldn't talk to the police, but many knew you were set up."

"One of the guys knew that your accuser Beth was living in Florida. From what I heard the owners bought her a condo in Florida, and one of the horse owners set her up with a job as a payroll clerk in one of his businesses."

She continued, "It took some time, but I found Beth was living near a horse track down there. I cased her schedule and found out she worked out almost every night at a gym near her home. I arranged to "bump" into her at the gym, and soon we were regular Zumba participants together. One thing led to another, and we started going out together."

"I gave her a story that I was only seventeen, with a real strict mother who recently threw me out. I guess I'm a pretty good liar dad, because she invited me to sleep on her couch for a few days. I shared how I would "do anything" to make money, and Beth said she may be able to help me."

"Beth told me that she wasn't doing it anymore. She muttered something about she had to lie and hurt someone who was good to her. But she had a friend who hooked girls up with rich horse owners in Florida. I played dumb and looked horrified dad. I asked if I had to sleep with the old guys."

And then Sophia recounted her conversation with Beth to Steven………

"Not necessarily," Beth said, "Some guys just like you around them. But I won't lie, the real money is in sex. It's not so bad. They pay up to

$2,000 a night. You get to go to nice restaurants and parties at the track. It's fun."

Again, playing dumb, Sophia asked, "Does it matter that I'm only seventeen?"

"Not at all," Beth laughed, "You're almost legal. Anyway some guys like 'em young. In fact my friend Rachel goes to high schools in Florida to recruit young girls. She sends the girls all over the country."

"Wow, this sounds like easy money. Can you set me up?"

"I don't do the parties anymore Sophia. I got a boyfriend who's a jockey. He doesn't want me doing that. But I could set you up with my friend Rachel if you're interested."

"Definitely. I need the money."..................

Sophia explained, "Dad, what Beth didn't know was that I recorded this whole conversation. I thought the F.B.I. might be interested. And dad, I was right. They had been trying to build a case against Jim Caldwell and the other owners for a long time. But these owners threw enough money around, like they did with Beth, to shut people up."

"The Miami F.B.I. Director David Adams was very interested in my tape. He said that while the tape was not admissible in Court, they had enough evidence to get a wiretap. They just needed a person to get inside the operation. And that was me dad," said a proud Sophia. "I wore a wire."

Steven squeezed his daughter's hands tightly. "That was a very brave thing to do." After a moment he haltingly asked, "Sophia, did you go to those parties with the girls?"

"Yes, dad, but nothing happened. I made myself throw up before a fat guy could touch me."

"Hold on," said a relieved Steven. "So what happened?"

"Well, I had training sessions with the F.B.I. The agents showed me what and what not to say and do. Wearing the wire was easy. None of the owners suspected anything. I met this girl Rachel, and because of Beth's recommendation she welcomed me with open arms. She told me I had to dress a bit sexier but kept saying the men would adore me. I got her on tape saying my age is no problem. She told me some of the girls are only sixteen, and the guys like them young. She even said some guys will pay more for a virgin, so she tells the girls to lie."

"They get the girls to ask their high school friends if they want to make easy money. And many say yes. And then they get the girls living on their own, and needing to pay rent. She said I wouldn't believe how easy it is to recruit a lot of different girls."

"Well, now that I was "in" my first party was at Paradise Racetrack in Miami. Early in the morning five of us girls had a spa day, followed by professional hair and makeup. Rachel even picked out the dresses we had to wear. It was like a wedding day. Then, after a day of big stakes races, Rachel had us picked up in a limousine and taken to some private golf club. The F.B.I. had fitted me with a watch that could record anything I wanted. With some practice, dad, I could tape a fly on a wall."

"Jim Caldwell and four other owners showed up, and they were pretty liquored up. They gave us martini's, which I drank very slowly. After dinner the guys picked out the girls they wanted. My guy was all belly with a bright red face. It didn't take long for the girls to start making out with the men. Things got pretty wild, as two of the girls took off their bras, and the men started hooting and hollering."

A concerned Steven asked, "So what happened to you honey?"

"I taped most of what I had to do before my beefy owner asked me to sit on his lap. Almost instinctively I turned and quickly put my fingers down my throat. Up came the crab appetizers that the waiters had served us. You know I never liked fish dad, especially crab. I threw up all over the guy's blue seersucker suit! I managed to say I was so sorry before I vomited again. The disgusted owner ran into the bathroom as the party stopped. All eyes turned to stare at me and the spittle on my face. Soon I heard Jim Caldwell call Rachel and yell, "Get this girl out of here, and get another girl here pronto!"

By now a relieved Steven and his daughter were laughing under a constellation of stars. Steven, still laughing said, "So you threw up on this rich owner? He must have wanted to kill you."

"If looks could kill dad, he would have. But they all got what they deserved in the end."

"So what happened after that?"

"David Adams was almost giddy when he saw the data on the tapes I made. He told me their weakest link was Beth Allen. Faced with almost twenty years in prison, Beth agreed to become the prime informant for the operation. She revealed details no one even knew about. Like one of the girls died from an overdose that the owners had supplied. Rachel had offered me some drugs to make me relax for my first party. She said that some girls work better with a little Percocet."

"And that's it dad. David Adams was instrumental in convincing the D.A.'s office to reconsider the charges against you. The only regret Beth shared with the F.B.I. about the conspiracy was your rape charge."

Sophia shared with her dad Beth's confession as was told to the F.B.I……..

"They had to drug me up to do what I did. Mr. Ricci would never touch me. Me and him bonded over our love of horses. Those rich assholes made me lie. Even when I was in that condo they bought me, I could never enjoy it. I felt dirty for what I had done to Mr. Ricci."

When he heard the words Beth had spoken, Steven cried, "That poor girl."

Chapter 26: The Best Years Until...

AT HOME IN THE WYOMING PRAIRIE Steven savored the next four years of his life. His son Steven Jr. shared his love of horses. By age fifteen, Steven Jr. was a skilled horseman. His favorite activity was taking his horse Apollo into the orange desert at daybreak and running wild with the Mustangs.

Juanita continued her vigilance to keep the Sanctuary financially stable. Steven's earlier hard work with legislators around the country produced a positive outcome. More states funded their own horse sanctuaries, which lessened the pressure on the Ricci's to take in so many retired thoroughbreds. In addition, many states banned the sale of horses for slaughter. Like Steven people were horrified at the fate of these thoroughbreds.

Steven became the happiest "mucker" on the planet. Each day he pampered his horses with the finest oats and barley, and occasional cubes of sugar. Racing fans and horse lovers toured the facility by the Snake River eager to talk to the once famous trainer and adore his retired horses. Steven declined the many entreaties he received from other owners to return to the sport as a trainer. "I couldn't be in a happier place," he would tell them. Each day he awakened with a kiss for Juanita to thank her for standing by him. In fact except for a few trips testifying to legislators and concerned citizens, he rarely left the Sanctuary. "Why would I want to be anywhere else?"

For her part Sophia fulfilled her dream rigorously pursuing her degrees to become a veterinarian. The F.B.I. had encouraged Sophia to consider changing her identity following her testimony against Jim Caldwell and ten other defendants. Her F.B.I. coordinator David Adams warned her, "These are dangerous people Sophia. They are wealthy and powerful. They might seek revenge."

But Sophia would have none of it. Her testimony, and that of the other star witness Beth Allen years earlier had riveted the country. The public learned that some of its esteemed business leaders were in reality sexual deviants. Newspaper headlines decreed: "Horse Owners Engaged in Sexual Conspiracy", "Girls, Many Underage, Trafficked Throughout the Country," "Horse owners Sent Recruiters to High Schools."

The owners' attorneys blasted the prosecution's charges as "fraudulent," and "trumped up". They tore into Beth's and Sophia's testimonies claiming that their clients had been framed. They accused the young girls of aggressively soliciting these men, posing as adult women who were essentially prostitutes. The jury later recounted that all of the young women were credible.

Jim Caldwell's attorney savagely cross-examined the prosecution's star witness Beth Allen:

"Isn't it true that all of you women were adults who enjoyed being in the company of these men?"

She calmly answered, "Yes, we were in the company of these men, but we didn't enjoy anything. We were coerced with money and even threatened by your client that we would lose our jobs at the track if we didn't attend these 'parties'. I was only seventeen at the time, and I needed that job."

Beth Allen later testified that Mr. Caldwell asked her to send some "filly's" to the after race party. The prosecution asked her to define "filly".

"Well, Mr. Caldwell wanted the girls from high school."

"So the defendant knew the girls were underage Ms. Allen?"

"Yes."

The defense again attacked the composed Ms. Allen like bloodthirsty mosquitos. "You know you were at a racetrack. Isn't it likely my clients were discussing horses?"

"I know the difference between young girls and horses."

A barrage of questions from the defense followed, but Beth was unruffled, and outspoken. "Yes we smiled at the parties, but we didn't enjoy them." "No, we were not adult women looking for a good time with men we knew had money." "No, we were not prostitutes."

On one such legal hankering Beth said, "These men even gave me drugs and made me wrongly accuse a man I respect, Steven Ricci of rape. He did no such thing." The attorneys got this stricken from the record, but the truth was heard by all.

The jury then watched the undercover tape of Sophia Ricci. One Rachel Watson is seen and heard saying, "Age is no problem," "We recruit high school girls," and "You would not believe how easy it is to recruit them." Unfortunately, they had to rely on the tape as Rachel Watson was not available to testify.

David Adams had told Sophia, "I hope Rachel is okay. They probably got to her somehow. It makes your testimony even more important."

Sophia Ricci then withstood ten hours of grueling cross examination. The lead defense attorney practically leaped out of his chair and pronounced sarcastically, "Isn't it true Ms. Ricci, that you did this escapade to free your dad from rape charges?"

Sophia answered calmly, "I did it to find out the truth, and that is what happened."

Her credibility was challenged, even to the point of her past allegations against her father. The Judge ruled quickly that, "Her testimony as a child is not part of this case."

Every attempt by the defense to rip into her agenda, accusing her of trying to free her dad and frame the horse owners failed. Why? The jurors squirmed in their seats when Sophia's video tapes with Beth Allen and Rachel were played. Two young looking girls are seen discussing, "sex parties" and the making of "easy money." One juror shook her head as Rachel is seen saying, "We go to high schools to recruit young girls."

The tapes were buttressed by a parade of young women who discussed their experiences with the owners. Some sobbed as they testified. "I felt I didn't have a choice," said one. Another said she lied about her age because, "It was easy money. I realize now it was not easy on my soul."

Steven Ricci sat with Juanita during the grueling days of Sophia's testimony. In fact he was there for the whole trial. One day Beth approached Steven outside the courtroom. She had her head down, unable to make eye contact with him. She asked for Steven's forgiveness. Steven moved close, "Look at me Beth. I know you did not want to do this. I forgive you and want you to come to my Sanctuary in Wyoming. You're welcome to stay as long as you want."

Steven was also in Court when the Jury reached a decision after two days of deliberations. All eight defendants were found guilty of federal sex trafficking charges. This included human trafficking of both adults and minors by use of "fraud, force and coercion." As leader of the conspiracy Jim Caldwell was sentenced to twenty years in prison despite his attorney's protestation of "a travesty of justice." Steven watched Jim Caldwell's tearful relatives as he was led out of the courtroom in handcuffs. Jim never made eye contact with his old trainer, preferring to sneer in the Judge's direction.

The other seven defendants received sentences of five to ten years based on their degree of participation in the conspiracy. As the rich men were similarly handcuffed Steven turned to Juanita and whispered, "Let's go home to Wyoming. It stinks in here."

The next two years were the happiest of Steven's life. Steven Jr. shared his dad's ability to communicate with horses. In fact, he now rode a Mustang that the Sanctuary staff had found in the desert with an injured leg. When healed, the wild horse refused to go back to its herd. It preferred its new home. Steven Jr. now roamed the prairie bareback on his friend.

Sophia was a frequent visitor to the Sanctuary in between her studies. Her horse acumen even now helped reduce the facility's vet fees. When she said, "I think I would like to be a horse surgeon," it was music to Steven's ears.

Another frequent visitor to the Sanctuary was Steven's mother Carole. She too marveled at the swaying grass severed by the Snake River wielding its way around the majestic mountains. "I love it here Steven," she said. She visited this beautiful place alone, since she was unable to entice her husband to leave his buddies.

One night as Steven and Carole sat alone on the veranda, Carole talked about Steven's father. "Remember that story I told you about your father?"

"Yeah, Mom."

"I'm glad you never did anything about that."

Steven's face turned so ashen, his mother instinctively knew something was wrong. "What is it Steven? What did you do?"

Her tone caused the guilt in Steven to surge. For a moment he hesitated, unsure if he should tell anyone, even his mom. But then the words tumbled out like the flowing Snake River after a storm. It felt good to relieve himself of this terrible secret.

His mom's face registered shock, anger, and dismay over the next ten minutes.

Steven scrutinized his mother's reaction, "I didn't want it to happen Ma, I swear."

Mother and son initially sat stunned under the black canvas surrounding the veranda. Steven broke the silence, "You must never tell anyone what I just told you Mom. Do you promise?"

"Yes," she said haltingly as she grabbed Steven's hand. She did not have the energy to say anything else. She was once again a despairing twenty year old widow with a son in diapers.

***

A year later Steven had pretty much forgotten that night. Wyoming, with all of its beauty, both natural and horse related, quickly collapses terrible memories. That is until the day a sheriff's vehicle wound its way up the Big House's dusty driveway. Two men in badges exited the vehicle and approached an apprehensive Juanita.

"Is Steven Ricci here?"

Steven heard his wife's voice call him as he bathed a new rescue. Juanita hoped he did not hear her. As Steven walked toward the group he immediately recognized the grim faces of law enforcement. Waving official looking papers at him, one of the officers asked, "Are you Steven Ricci?"

Steven nodded apprehensively.

"We have an arrest warrant for you, for the murder of Nicolas Bianco Jr." Steven dropped his head. Juanita had seen this defeated look before. Steven then put his hands behind his back.

Chapter 27: The Secret

FOR THE THIRD TIME Steven Ricci found himself in a familiar place: behind bars where he rightfully belonged. For if he was framed in his previous two imprisonments, that was not the case now. No, he had killed Nicky Bianco Jr. The reason was still as much a mystery to Steven as when it happened two years earlier. At that time he had diverted from a horse rescue trip to a small racetrack in northern California. He wanted to find the source of Nicky's vitriol against him all these years; and to test a family secret that united these two fatherless men.

First, he had to come clean to his tearful daughter and his solemn wife who sat behind the polluted window in the county jail. Sophia sobbed, "Dad, please tell me you didn't do it. You promised me you wouldn't retaliate against Nicky for my testimony years ago." Juanita did not need to hear Steven's answer. She had seen the familiar wounded expression on her husband before.

Steven explained to his daughter, "I did not mean to kill him. This had nothing to do with that business years ago. " He gulped hard, "You see I have been living with a secret that involves Nicky and me. My mother told me this a few years ago and swore me to secrecy. The racetrack pipeline made me aware that Nicky was down and out living at a racetrack outside of San Francisco. I wanted to talk to him about our fathers."

For the next hour the women dabbed at their eyes as they listened to Steven reveal the events of that sad day two years earlier. This secret that had reverted him to the Steven of old – the selfish person who used others for his own gain. In this case, to stay out of prison.

"You see Nicky's father, Nicky Sr. and my father, Phillip, were once best friends. My mother used to say they were, "Thick as thieves who preferred hanging around the racetrack instead of going to school." She told me they weren't bad kids, but they had their share of legal trouble. They both quit high school on the same day."

"My mother said all that changed after their double date. Nicky Sr. had been dating my Mom. Nicky asked my father to join him and my Mom on a double date with her best friend Connie, who was rather shy. Well, something happened on that date. My Mom called it instant chemistry between my her and my dad."

"One thing led to another, and my Mom dropped Nicky and started dating my dad. She recognized my dad had bigger plans for his life, plans that included her. Nicky was always just out for a good time, and he scared her when he was intoxicated, which was often. My father realized his friend was going down a bad path. My father chose to join the Marines because he knew he needed discipline in his life. He even secured his G.E.D."

"Nicky Sr. never got over my Mom's rejection. My dad felt terrible, and at first he told Nicky he would stop dating my Mom. But he couldn't stay away from her. Nicky's response was to shun the couple. My parents married a year later. Both were only nineteen years old. A year after that my father was sent to Vietnam."

"So my dad was overjoyed when, on a leave from Vietnam, his old friend Nicky called him. He told my dad that he couldn't reject a guy that was fighting to save his ass. Nicky also shared that he was a father to one year old Nicky Jr. Although he hadn't married Nicky Jr.'s mom, he planned to do it soon. The old friends made plans for a day at their favorite racetrack. My Mom warned my dad that she heard Nicky was running with a rough crowd, and even may be dealing drugs. My dad, confident in his Marine uniform, just laughed it off. He actually thought he might straighten Nicky out. Ironically, I was conceived on this leave."

"Later that day my Mom got an excited call from my dad. He was thrilled to tell her he had just hit a pick six bet at the races for $28,000. They could now put a down payment on a home. My mom told me she was concerned when he made a comment about Nicky.

I remember the words she told me my father said, "You're right Carole. Nicky is not the same guy. I'll tell you all about it when I get home."

Steven continued, "Several hours later a grim faced police officer and a Marine adjutant were at my Mom's doorstep. They told her my dad had been killed in his car in a terrible accident not far from the racetrack. The car had flown off a rural mountainside road, bulleting through brush and finally crashing into a large oak tree. My mother collapsed to the floor. When she regained consciousness her first question was, "Where was Nicky? The officer answered that Phillip was alone. Her next question was, "Did he have any money on him?" The officer's answer was, "No."

Steven paused to let his daughter and wife take in all that he had said.

"Think about all the challenges my mother had to navigate. She found herself sleepwalking through a year of grief; planning a funeral, living as a widow, and finally the joy and sadness of giving birth to me. She told me three months after my birth two officials came to her door. As I played at her feet she listened to the events that had deprived me of a father……………………

The officer explained, "Phillip was not killed in the accident. He had been stabbed, probably by Nicky Bianco. The medical examiner found two stab wounds near his heart. We think the accident was staged by Nicky to cover up the murder. The motive was robbery. We confirmed your husband had in fact won $28,000 as you said."

"This goes deeper than money," uttered Carole.

The officials had a second bombshell. "Nicky Bianco is also dead. He was found two weeks after your husband's death in a drug den outside of Chicago. He was flashing money around. Someone probably gave him a bad smack and robbed him."

Little Steven's future was then negotiated as he played with his toys. The adjutant spoke, "Carole, we recommend we leave the death certificate as is, death by car accident. You and your son can receive full Marine benefits until Steven is eighteen. That might be jeopardized if there is an investigation when no one really knows what happened. Nicky had a son, Nicky Jr., who is about two years old. The mother, one Vivian Knowlton, alleges the old friends were both using drugs.

Gazing down at her happy one year old son playing with blocks Carol nodded her head in affirmation.

Catching breaths to absorb this sordid story Juanita finally spoke, “This is a terrible story. But why did you have to go to California to find Nicky? Didn’t you think about Steven Jr.? He needs a father too,” she said angrily.

“You’re right Juanita, and I’ve beat myself up for two years for deciding to go there. I guess I wanted to know why he hated me so much. I wanted to know what his family told him about what happened. I just wanted him to know the truth. I even had some crazy idea that I could help him, maybe get him sober at the Sanctuary. I wanted to end this family trauma.”

Finally Sophia asked, “So what happened dad?”

“When I saw Nicky, I didn’t even recognize him. He weighed about a hundred pounds. His skin was pale, and his eyes were dull and hollow. His thin arms were all black and blue. I heard that some trainer took pity on him and let him stay in a horse stall on the backside. He recognized me immediately, and his voice was horse when he asked, “What are you doing here?”

“I told him I wanted to help him. I asked if he knew our fathers were best friends. He told me to leave him alone, that he didn't care about me or my fucking father. Juanita, I swear I started walking away, but I turned at the stall exit. I said, "Nicky, I know your father killed my father, but I forgive him. We both lost our fathers that day."

"With that Nicky's burnt out eyes grew wide, and he charged at me with power no one hundred pound skeleton should possess. He screamed, "Forgive who? It was your dad who robbed and killed my father! He stole $28,000 from my father and killed him. And now I'm going to kill you!"

Steven closed his eyes while revealing the next five minutes and his own near death. "At first I was deflecting Nicky's punches, but then I realized something shiny was in his hand. Those old jockey fingers had that knife five inches from my eyes at one point Juanita. I was in a fight for my life with a half dead lunatic. Somehow, I got the knife, but I don't even remember how. In a daze I reacted to Nicky's reign of punches and countered with one of my own. The next thing I knew blood was gushing out of his neck. Nicky fell back, his eyes fixated on me as I put a towel to his neck. I was screaming, "I'm sorry, I'm sorry." The tears streamed down Steven's face as he said, "Juanita, Nicky's angry eyes never left me."

Longing to take Steven into her arms and console him, Juanita was able only to put her hand against the soiled window that separated her husband from her and his daughter. Finally, Sophia spoke, "Dad, this was self-defense. Why didn't you just call the police?"

"I know, I know. But I'm a two time convicted loser. The old me returned. I ran away from the trouble I caused. I just wanted to get out of there. I saw an ornery horse in a nearby stall. I regret to this day what I did next. I dragged Nicky's body into the unruly horse's stall. I figured no one cared about a poor soul who got stomped on by a horse." Then somberly he added, "And I was right, but I've been in pain every day."

Juanita asked the inevitable question, "How did the police find out it was you, Steven?"

"Only one person knows I committed this murder, my mother Carole. I told her what I did to her old boyfriend's son. She had trusted me with the facts about my dad, so I figured it was the right thing to do."

Incredulous, Sophia demanded, "So it was your Mom who ratted you out?"

"Honey, do you remember when the F.B.I. wanted to place you in the Witness Protection Program? Jim Caldwell and his cronies got a more direct way for revenge. They have had plenty of time behind bars to find a way to get to me. I hear Carole's husband, my stepfather, is driving to his softball games in a brand new Escalade. I figure my Mom must have blurted something to him. The authorities exhumed Nicky's body and found my knife wounds."

The three sat in somber silence. Finally, Junita asked, "Your arraignment is tomorrow, Steven. What are you going to do?"

Steven revealed his soul searching truth, "I may not be guilty of intentionally killing Nicky, but it would not have happened if I left the secret dead. And I hid the crime in a terrible way. Nicky did not deserve that and I'll never forgive myself for not calling the police that night. I was innocent in my first two imprisonments, but not now."

Juanita sobbed, and Sophia sadly shook her head as Steven informed them, "I'm pleading guilty tomorrow. Morris thinks we can combine all the charges -including voluntary manslaughter, obstruction of justice, and abuse of a corpse in a plea deal. No more than a six year sentence. Juanita, with good time, I'll be out in three years. Will you wait for me, you and Steven Jr.?"

"Of course," she answered as Steven placed both his palms on the glass to meet her own.

At his sentencing hearing, after pleading guilty and receiving the six year sentence, Steven told the Judge, "I apologize to Mr. Bianco's family for the pain I caused them." Ironically, the only family who heard the sorrowful words were Sophia, and one of Nicky's old girlfriends. Neither Sophia's mother Alyssa, nor Damien Bianco were present. Sophia had correctly predicted that no family would show up.

Following the sentencing hearing the Judge allowed the Ricci family to say their goodbyes in a nearby conference room. Steven, Juanita, and Sophia cried and hugged for what seemed like an eternity.

Steven finally broke the silence. "Sophia honey, how did you know no one would show up for the hearing?"

"Well I wasn't sure about Damien. No one knows where he is. He's nineteen and last I heard he was living in Las Vegas. When Mom married Pat Williams she simply was happy to be a dentist's wife and live quietly in Calvert, a small town near Sacramento."

"After Damien was born things between Nicky and Mom were okay. Nicky was winning races everywhere and was away a lot. Damien adored his dad and ran around the house on a stick with a horse's head saying I'm going to be a jockey just like my daddy. Nicky would take us to the backside and Damien would always be on his dad's shoulders."

"Everything changed when Damien was about four. Nicky fractured his back in a race at Templeton. He couldn't ride for over a year. He got hooked on pain medication, and sat on the couch drinking and yelling at Mom. When he got better and tried to return, he had trouble making weight and tested positive for cocaine. He lost his jockey license and things just got worse and worse."

"You know Dad, Nicky would sit on the couch in a drug induced haze threatening to blow up the house with us in it. We were all so scared, but Damien took it the worst. He would say, 'Daddy, daddy, don't hurt us.' Nicky slapped me once and said I deserved it with a father like you."

"After another violent night of Nicky's drunken rants, he tried to leave the gas stove on with no flame. Mom took us that night and we never returned or saw Nicky again. We spent that first night in a car. We eventually went to Mom's parents' for a while. Mom met Pat Williams when I was nine and Damien was six. He's such a great guy Dad. He treated us like his own. You would love him. We moved to the wonderful town of Calvert where Pat had a good dental practice. We had a good life there and Mom is so happy. I think she just wants to forget all the ugliness of her past."

Steven asked, "How did Damien handle the divorce and not seeing his dad?"

"Not good. Damien seemed to take his anger out on everyone, especially Mom. He blamed her for Nicky's problems. Every Christmas he waited for a gift from Nicky that never came. Damien rebelled in school and had fights with everyone. When he assaulted a teacher trying to break up one of his fights, he was expelled. Mom and Pat spent thousands of dollars on therapy for him. At fifteen Damien was sent to a Military Academy where he was soon expelled for using Marijuana. Then he was sent to an alternative high school, and again expelled. He left home at eighteen. Mom hired a private detective to find him, and that's when we found out he was living in Las Vegas for a while. He had been arrested for dealing drugs. He skipped bail and no one has heard from him since. Mom is heartbroken. She blames herself."

The room was quiet again until the door slammed. Two burly guards announced, "Time's up, Ricci."

"Thank you, guys, for this time," said Steven as he hugged his family. He whispered his last words to Sophia, "Maybe we can get Damien out to the Sanctuary. The horses will heal him."

Before he left for prison Steven was granted one last meeting with his son. He asked Steven Jr. to take care of Juanita. Steven Jr. will always remember his dad's words:

"I'm very proud of you son. Please always stay the humble, respectful, and honest person you are. I've failed sometimes in the past in those qualities, but I've changed. I'm not that way now."

All Steven Jr. could say was, "Just come home safe Dad. I'll have Max waiting for you."

Upon arrival at Lennox one guard greeted him, "Can't stay out of this place, huh."

In fact when you are a third timer in a prison there is a certain sympathy and respect for you, especially if you are a former celebrity with an unusual prison history. So the old timers who would never get out of prison welcomed Steven back.

"Three years is a piece of cake," said the aging Mafioso who also added, "You got your old job back in the library."

After a year in prison, Steven still followed the same routine every day. He got up to say his morning prayers, and then put an "X" on the calendar.

One thing that helped pass the time was a reading program for young prisoners Steven had started in the library. These young men who brought years of frustrated learning were the candidates he recruited. A small group began reading sixth grade books. The characters and plots soon consumed them and became a springboard to more complex discussions.

Abandoned children in one story led a young prisoner to ask, “How could a parent just leave these kids? They didn’t ask to be born.”

Bad educators in another story led a prisoner to share, “One teacher told me I would never amount to anything.”

Word of mouth led to larger classes and the need for a larger library, which Steven solicited. As time went on many of his supposedly “dumb” prisoners were reading the Iliad, Catcher in the Rye, and naturally Seabiscuit. And the discussions gave the prisoners an outlet for sharing which was a new experience for them.

This program helped Steven to forgive himself. He grew to accept that indeed he was a good person, despite his failings on that terrible night. *When I get out of here, I’ll make sure someone takes over this library program,* he thought.

But the night Steven fell asleep watching the spider create his spectacular web of a prison within a prison was a difficult one. Semi-asleep he recalled his childhood days, many spent abusing his classmates and teachers. He thought about how he had turned on Pops when offered the chance to advance himself. His sleeplessness evoked bad memories of the son who tormented his Mom. The one good thought was that Carole was now living at the horse sanctuary, unable to live with her husband who had betrayed Steven.

Steven tried to abort the bad memories, visualizing the undulating grasses shifting on the Wyoming plains. But he could not block out these painful recollections. This night was dominated by the old Steven, who left Nicky alone to be trampled in a horse stall.

Reality set in the next morning. Steven felt good about himself after he said his prayers. He put an "X" on the calendar and called for the guard. Today he was meeting a new batch of convicts anxious to start reading sixth grade books. His head busy thinking about which books to introduce to the young prisoners, Steven was not aware of his drab surroundings. He did not see the stout prisoner wearing a black durag veering into his path. Steven heard the words, but felt no pain. Someone whispered in his ear, "Damien Bianco says hello." A thin shiv ripped up Steven's abdomen. The killer then formed a "T" on Steven's torso by cutting a second time. The slaying happened so quickly that the killer was able to seamlessly join the hungry prisoners for breakfast.

Epilogue

JUANITA KNEW IT WAS crazy mind talk, but initially she was angry at Steven for leaving her. He had promised he would return to her, Steven Jr., and the Wyoming plains. He vowed he'd return to their life at the Sanctuary, surrounded by free roaming horses and mountains and prairies as far as the eye could see.

Juanita, Carole, and Steven Jr. absorbed the prison phone call that now diminished these dreams forever. The Warden said the doctors tried to save Steven, but the hemorrhaging blood prevailed over the feverishly working doctors. The Warden told Juanita that Steven's last words were, "I'm sorry."

The unfinished murder investigation into the killer and the alleged role of Damien did not matter to Juanita. All that mattered was that the love of her life was gone. A fact even the Sanctuary horses seemed to understand, their coats no longer shining by Steven's tender care.

One evening at twilight Steven Jr., Juanita, Carole and Owen mounted head dropping stallions and set out onto the plains with a purpose. The setting sun bathed the Snake River and rolling hills with crisp orange hues. The group saw a herd of Mustangs coming toward them.

Steven Jr. was carrying the precious box which contained Steven's ashes. He had once told his family, "I want to be let out with the horses just like Pops." The lead Mustang galloped toward the four souls before him, then paused on a dime and snorted in the group's direction, a cloud of dust enveloping everyone. Steven Jr. turned the box upside down, the ashes flying in the Mustang's direction. As if reacting to the event, the Mustang stomped the ground, then reared back on his hind legs aggressively. Seeing no movement from these bereaved interlopers the lead Mustang, content he had withstood any challenge, galloped away, the rest of the herd in pursuit.

Retreating to the Sanctuary the four horsemen were enveloped in silence. But one mind was quite active. Steven Jr. silently vowed he would avenge his father's murder. As if reading her son's mind, Juanita pulled her horse to a stop.

"Steven please promise me that this violence stops here. Your dad regretted his act of retribution every day."

Unable to look his mother in the eye, Steven Jr. said, "Okay Mom, I promise."

www.ingramcontent.com/pod-product-compliance
Lightning Source LLC
Chambersburg PA
CBHW050410260626
47156CB00003B/948

* 9 7 8 1 6 3 8 6 8 1 8 7 8 *